The Gregg Press
Science Fiction Series

David G. Hartwell and L. W. Currey, *Editors*

Sunburst
by Phyllis Gotlieb

Sunburst

PHYLLIS GOTLIEB

With a New Introduction by
ELIZABETH A. LYNN

GREGG PRESS

A DIVISION OF G. K. HALL & CO., BOSTON, 1978

This is a complete photographic reprint of a work first published in Greenwich, Connecticut by Fawcett Publications, Inc. in 1964.

The trim size of the original paperback edition was 4¼ by 7⅛ inches.

Text copyright © 1964 by Fawcett Publications, Inc.
Reprinted by arrangement Berkley Publishing Corp.
Introduction copyright © 1978 by Elizabeth A. Lynn

Frontispiece photograph of Phyllis Gottlieb courtesy of the author's agent.

Printed on permanent/durable acid-free paper and bound in the United States of America.

Republished in 1978 by Gregg Press, A Division of G. K. Hall & Co., 70 Lincoln St., Boston, Massachusetts 02111

First Printing, December, 1978

Library of Congress Cataloging in Publication Data

Gotlieb, Phyllis Bloom.
   Sunburst.

   (The Gregg Press science fiction series)
   This ed. first published in 1964 by Fawcett
Publications, Greenwich, Conn.
   Includes bibliographical references.
   I. Title. II. Series.
PZ4.G68Su 1978 [PR9199.3.G64]   813'.5'4   78-21597
ISBN 0-8398-2500-5

Introduction

Sunburst began in my mind around 1955 as a short story about a girl with psi who was gradually lured into the Dump because she could find no other persons like herself. She was a twelve-year-old then, but *Lolita* came out and the phrase "twelve-year-old-girl" took on connotations I didn't want, so I gave her another year. . . . It occurred to me she'd be more interesting if she *didn't* have psi. . . . A short story didn't seem long enough for [this idea]. . . . By then it was April 1960, and the original short story never did get written. *Sunburst* was finished December 1961 . . . and first bought by Cele Goldsmith (Lalli) . . . in May 1963 as an *Amazing* serial; and then by Fawcett, February 1964.[1]

Phyllis Gotlieb

PHYLLIS GOTLIEB'S first published SF short story, "A Grain of Manhood" was also bought by Cele Goldsmith. It appeared in *Fantastic,* September 1959. *Sunburst* was published in *Amazing* in March–May, 1964. Phyllis Gotlieb was then, as now, living in Toronto, Canada. She is married, with three children. She is not well-known to SF readers, possibly because she is Canadian, possibly because her body of work is small. She has written four books of poetry. In reviewing the second, *Ordinary, Moving, Library Journal* called her "one of the best Canadian poets now at work."[2] Her poem "Dr. Umlaut's Earthly Kingdom" was broadcast in 1970 by the CBC and can be found in the CBC publication *Poems For Voices.* She has had 13 short stories published to date in U.S. SF magazines. Three of these have been reprinted. She has published two SF novels: *Sunburst,* originally a Fawcett paperback, now available from Berkley, and *O Master Caliban!* (Harper & Row, 1976.) *O Master Caliban!* will be available from Bantam in 1979. She is currently working on a third science fiction novel. She writes: ". . . I am a . . . slow writer. SF has been my main work for over twenty years. . . ."

She has written one mainstream novel about the survivor of a Nazi concentration camp: *Why Should I Have All The Grief?* (Macmillan of Canada, 1969). She writes of that experience: "People kept urging me to write a mainstream novel, and I wrote one to see if I could. It took four years, got quite a few good reviews, sold about 700 copies, and brought in $407.79. I think it was quite a good book, and it taught me a lot, but the lesson was too expensive." That novel is unavailable in the U.S. and is now out of print in Canada.[3] *Sunburst* survives. Counting translations, this Gregg Press edition is its 11th publication.

Sunburst deals emphatically and directly with moral issues. Gotlieb writes that it was not an easy book to sell: ". . . I have a nice sheaf of rejection letters declaring it to be depressing, over-compressed, poorly-organized, [and] uninteresting because the protagonist is a thirteen-year-old girl. . . ." The science fiction market fifteen years ago consisted largely of young men scarcely out of their teens. Though historically science fiction—from Mary Shelley's *Frankenstein* (1818) to Ursula K. Le Guin's *The Dispossessed* (1974)—is one of the most effective genres for focusing on questions of human responsibility, a large number of the SF books on the market are still written for an audience that looks for entertainment without philosophy, preferring colorful adventure and sanitized romance to genuine literary exploration. This was truer 30 years ago; it grows less true as SF grows farther away from its pulp magazine origins. The blurb on the front cover of the Fawcett edition of *Sunburst* exemplifies what publishers believed would attract an SF audience in 1964: "A fiendish race of demonic children is spawned in the genetic chaos of a runaway reactor explosion." There is no suggestion that this book is more than a stereotypical SF adventure. The blurb itself is a remarkable perversion of the novel's plot.

Sunburst is about children. Specifically, it considers the nature of the relationship between a "normal" society and its supernormal children. The silly phrase "demonic children" evokes a list of popular titles: Thompson's *Lupe* (1977), McCammon's *Baal* (1978), Blatty's *The Exorcist* (1971), Levin's *Rosemary's Baby* (1967). These books are often lumped together with science fiction titles in bookstore racks, as if they were one genre. We will return later to this consideration. For the moment it suffices to point out that science fiction's demonic children are less literal than metaphorical. Science fiction transmutes the theme of the supernormal into that of the alien or the mutant.

One example of the former is John Wyndham's *The Midwich Cuckoos,* out of which was made the 1960 movie (screenplay by Sterling Silliphant), *Village of the Damned.* In this novel (published in 1958) all the women of an English country town are made pregnant by a mysterious force. They give birth to aliens: identical blond and golden-eyed children with a communal intelligence and frightening mental powers. At the conclusion of the story it is clear that the children are not human and they are destroyed. Aliens are dangerous *because* they are alien. Nonhumans are not members of the social contract.

In the wake of the Manhattan Project, a number of SF novels were written about or around mutation. The theme lends itself to two distinct treatments. The first sees the mutant as inevitably separate from the human race, possessed of its own needs and its own morality, with no more responsibility to its parent than a virus has to the body of its host. In Frank M. Robinson's classic book *The Power* (1956), which also had a rather unfaithful movie version, the mutant Adam Hart treats the "normal" human beings he encounters as toys, things to be manipulated and then destroyed. When the hero and protagonist William Tanner discovers that he, too, is a mutant, his "human" morality falls away from him as easily as a discarded blanket. A similar treatment, with a different emotional slant, can be seen in Arthur C. Clarke's remarkable novel *Childhood's End* (1953).

The second treatment of the theme assumes the mutant to be—as does Clarke—the next "step" in the development of human evolution, but still part of the human race, responsible to it and for it. In *Childhood's End* the acts of the mutant children are morally *sui generis.* In stories which see the mutant as not *too* different from the nonmutant, the acts of the mutant towards "normals," and vice versa, are judged by the standards of the social contract. Wyndham's *Re-Birth* (1955) falls into this category, as does Wilmar Shiras' novel *Children of the Atom* (1953). A clear example of this treatment can be found in Theodore Sturgeon's brilliant *More Than Human* (1953). Sturgeon depicts a group of supernormal people, and follows is Jason Hemmer, "Dumper's peeper," whose job it is to scout cipally concerned with survival in a world which neither understands them nor trusts them. As adults they perforce interact with their human neighbors. They do so erratically and sometimes viciously until they reach moral maturity. When they do, they realize that they are part of the next step in human evolution, and become the new entity, "homo gestalt."

An early novel which utilized the mutant vs. non-mutant theme is A. E. van Vogt's *Slan,* published in 1940. In it, the telepathic slans are a natural mutation destined to replace the current human model. "Normal" human beings hate slans, who in turn feel pity and loathing for human beings. The possibilities of kinship and mutual growth are not mentioned. Though the adventure is vivid and the characterization strong, the book seems dated now. It is still entertaining. But since Hiroshima SF has tended to treat the possibilities of mutation seriously, that is, recognizing the historical and emotional complexities in what was once only a dramatic assumption. *Slan* is less serious fiction than it is vigorous soap opera.

Sunburst, despite its cover copy, is not soap opera. Within the conventions of science fiction Gotlieb does some complex theatrical maneuvering. There are three sets of supernormal people in the fictional midwestern town of Sorrel Park. The first set is comprised of the Dumplings, the "demonic children" of the blurb. They are telepathic, telekinetic, and psychopathic. Created by the radiation from the blowup of a nuclear plant, they are juvenile delinquents, cruel and powerful, confined to their prison in the Dump by the Marzcinek Field, "a toroidal white-noise field that would scramble everything but light radiation. . ." (p. 43). . . . "Some crazy chance had decreed that when the psi mutation hit the human race it would choose the type of child most likely to develop the delinquent type of psychopathic personality. . . ." (p. 21). Their leader is Curtis Quimper. Their prominent members are LaVonne Hurley, "a dwarf with a twisted, compressed body and a mind equally ugly" (pp. 36–7); Colin Prothero, son of the colonel into whose charge the traumatized town is eventually put; Doydoy, a stammering genius who suffers from *spina bifida.* They hate the town, everything in it, and the world outside from which they have been barred for eight years.

The second set has three members: three telepaths who are not psychopathic and therefore not confined to the Dump. Two of them live in the town and are not known to be psis. The third

them from childhood to adulthood. As children they are prin-
the town of Sorrel Park "for new psis as they [are] born or more
likely, as their powers [develop] during childhood" (p. 7).

The final set is a single-member set: it consists of Shandy,
Sandra Ruth Johnson, the novel's protagonist. Shandy is thirteen, lanky and tall, curious, intelligent, and feisty. She also
possesses a startling talent. She is an Imper. Her mind is impervious to psi.

Sorrel Park, first because of the Blowup and then because of
the Dumplings, the imprisoned children, has lived under martial law for 30 years, long enough for its residents to have forgotten any experience of freedom. But Shandy, in a town ringed
with barbed wire and crawling with police, is a free spirit. She
has managed to avoid being pulled into the Dump to be
measured for psi—not in itself a frightening thing if you haven't
got it—without quite knowing why she has steered so very clear
of the place. She is "different;" she knows it, her foster mother
knows it, even the local bootlegger knows it when he tells Jason
Hemmer about her. Part of the difference lies in her talent:

"Most normal people have latent or vestigial psi. It's a lot stronger in
babies and little kids, but it's a kind of clumsy and inarticulate thing,
and it withers away when better methods of communication develop.
But adults can still feel the presence of people they can't see, most of
the time unconsciously, or nobody could ever hide. With you it's different. Anybody who notices you practically has to tread on your toes
first. I even have to concentrate hard before I can see you in anybody
else's mind." (p. 16)

Noticed by Hemmer, Shandy goes into the Dump for examination by Urquhart, the Dump's psychiatrist. Urquhart suggests to
Colonel Prothero that her talent might make her useful in dealing with the Dumplings. The adults within the Dump are
troubled, nearly desperate. After 30 years, there is talk about
Sorrel Park being "opened up."

A less sensitive writer might have chosen to make the Dumplings into The Enemy, thus removing moral tension from the
story and eliminating all internal conflict. But Gotlieb never lets
us forget that the Dumplings, though terrible, are human
children, entitled to the protection of the social contract. Thus
Jason Hemmer goes in among them, letting himself be beaten
while he learns which of them has physical injuries. The most
malicious of them, LaVonne, is accorded reasons for her
behavior and, with them, a measure of dignity:

"It's my body and I'm stuck with it. I can do anything I like but change my body, 'cause I can't be sure it'd keep workin' if I did. Roxy Howard tried it an' killed herself an' I'm not gonna be that kind of nut. But if you didn't have me pegged down like this I could do anything I liked with you. I could change those brains you're so uppity about into cheese or jelly or lead. Then you wouldn't think I was so ugly because you wouldn't be thinkin'." (p. 65–6)

As the adults grapple with the problem of Sorrel Park's eventual exposure, Shandy grapples with the problem of who and what she is. For 13 years she has been isolated and—she realizes—emotionally impervious to the turmoil of the town. Now, talking with Jason, with Dr. Marzcinek, with Dr. Grace Halsey, she finds herself growing vulnerable as her self-awareness expands. The two conflicts merge when the Dumplings escape. Doydoy, their spastic genius, has broken the Field for them. He vanishes. Shandy figures out where he is and takes Jason to him. He is in hiding from the Dumplings. Clearly superior to them in intellect, he loves and hates them, wishing to be free of them yet fearful of leaving the security of the only community he has known.

When the Dumplings find the three of them, Shandy is the only one who is free to act. As an Imper, she is resistant to the Dumplings' telepathic powers. Calmly she limns Doydoy's dilemma out, and gives him corresponding freedom to act: "I think Donatus ought to make his own choice" (p. 91). Doydoy vanishes, with Jason. Furious at the loss of them, Prothero orders Shandy to return to a place that now seems hopeless to her: the town outside the Dump. For the first time in her life Shandy has found a community, with Jason and Marzcinek and Grace Halsey, and she does not want to relinquish it.

Led by LaVonne, the Dumplings kidnap Marzcinek and take him to Chicago, where they know there is "an important computer." Inevitably Shandy is drawn into the final conflict with them. In the confrontation which follows, the Dumplings— tricked and manipulated by Doydoy—turn on each other. Colin Prothero, the colonel's son, is killed. LaVonne, Curtis Quimper and a few others of the original Pack survive.

As a result of the escape, Shandy learns, Sorrel Park is to be opened to the world. The town is being given its freedom. Also as a result of her involvement with the Dumplings, Shandy learns some necessary truths about herself—who she is, and why she is "different." She learns what she is free to do, and what that freedom implies.

In the books previously mentioned *(Slan, Re-Birth, The Power)* there is a tendency to assume that psionic powers imply or confer some kind of genetic superiority. This is not an unusual assumption in science fiction. It goes largely unexamined. It's interesting, therefore, to read what Gotlieb has to say about this in *Sunburst:*

People have always thought of psi as something superhuman. . . . You said once that most normal people have vestiges of it, telepathy, at least, but it's stronger in babies and kids because they can't express themselves very well by talking. . . . So if there's any everyday kind of psi it's telepathy in babies and kids . . . maybe herd animals, too, and ants? . . . When it finally came to people as a radiation mutation it hit juvenile delinquents. . . . What have they got in common? . . . Psychopaths have brainwaves like children. . . . *Their minds seem more primitively organized.* That's what they've got in common with all the other creatures in the world that have psi. . . (p. 114-5)

Shandy herself says about this that it's only an idea, and not meant to account for all the psis in Sorrel Park. She admits it doesn't account for Jason. It's not until the end of the book that she realizes, ironically, that her theory about the Dumplings can be stretched to tell her about her own place in the world. Urquhart asks her, under hypnosis, to describe what she thinks the Superman would be like, since telepathy, far from being an attribute of the supernormal, is a primitive talent—a step back. She answers:

". . . he has to be moral or he'll do harm. Urquhart: You want a person who's protected from the mischances of psychodynamic forces. Shandy: Yes. Somebody who'd turn out to be moral no matter what happened to him. . . . With plenty of room to be different." (p. 152)

Naively, she describes herself.

From our current sociological standpoints, the theories in *Sunburst* about the roots of juvenile deliquency[4] may be questionable. But in fact no one has yet discovered the "cause" of juvenile deliquency, and no one, of course, knows anything about the genetics of psi. Shandy's theory about telepathy may be perfectly correct: "The way telepathy turns up in animals it's . . . pretty clumsy. For herd animals that have to stick together it might be useful, but I bet a human being born with it could never separate his mind from everybody else's long enough to develop a logical idea." (p. 151). If psi does *inhibit,* not facilitate communication, then the logical Superman is impervious to its effects. Commenting upon this theory, Phyllis Gotlieb writes: "I don't know if it (telepathy) really exists; on the whole, for reasons of privacy, I hope not."

Sunburst, then, falls into the second category of books that deal with mutant vs. human conflict: the mutant (functional or dysfunctional) is part of the human race. The superman

". . . is a kind ordinary people could live with, even if they felt he was a little eccentric. He'd have the same emotions and the same hopes. . . . You couldn't expect an advance to come in a single impossible leap to the summit . . . His life might be hard and lonely, he might wish he weren't different at all—but I don't see how he could be really unhappy when he had the whole universe to observe and learn about and understand." (p. 153)

His task is not to rule the world but "to transfuse interesting and valuable new genes into humanity. . ." (p. 159). Scientifically and dramatically this is a reasonable conclusion. It affirms the essential humanity of the superman, and reaffirms faith in the future. It confirms the writer's and the readers' trust in the viability of the social contract.

Let us digress for a moment to compare this class of books—tales about superchildren—to current thrillers like *Damon* (1975) or *The Exorcist.* Even a cursory reading reveals one major difference. In the science fiction novels, children are seen, literally, as the next step in human evolution. Plots are pegged to science—or at least, to technology. The future is assumed to be possibly dangerous and probably complex but almost certainly hopeful. In thrillers like *The Exorcist,* plots are pegged to pseudopsychology or else to the supernatural, and children appear as monsters: demonic, psychotic, or possessed. The generations are estranged, and the future seems hostile and uncertain. It seems significant that in one of the most effective scenes in a recent thriller, Stephen King's *The Shining* (1977), a father goes after his telepathic son with an axe.

It may indicate distrust or disillusionment with the promises of technology, that popular fiction these days turns to the supernatural as easily as it turns to science. Whatever the cause, the effect is clear. The genre persists. It differs from science fiction structurally, as well as thematically. Like all genre fiction, it is limited by its own conventions. In thrillers where a child is "possessed," part of the horror in the possession comes from the fact that the character of the child—good, bad, thrifty, clean, courteous, reverent, whatever—is irrelevant to the possessing agent. Under such conditions external tensions are more important than internal i.e. moral, tension, and the details of the children's personalities are often barely sketched in.

Science fiction is often charged with substituting stereotypes for characters. This may be true at times (there are bad writers everywhere) but at least it is not one of the conventions of the genre. The Dumplings are not "possessed" by their psionic powers. Within the limits of intelligence and the physical strictures that surround them, they are free. In the bare artificial world of the Dump, moral acts have the inexorability of physical laws. In their misuse of their powers, they create their own destruction. Action implies reaction.

Gotlieb is careful to remind us, however, that in the world beyond the Dump the reaction is less precise. The good do not always prosper; right does not always prevail. Marzcinek, whom Shandy has learned to love, is badly hurt, perhaps dying, and Jason can offer her no comfort: ". . . He doesn't owe it to you to hang on just because you love him" (p. 158). There is a poignant moment at the close of the book. Curtis Quimper attempts to deflect LaVonne's malice, and is rewarded for this good impulse by freedom, of a sort: he is not reimprisoned behind the rebuilt Field. He and Shandy meet in the Dump library. Shandy asks him how he is. "Lonely," he answers. She says, "Bro-ther, you aren't the only one!" (p. 160).

Of all the characters in *Sunburst,* Shandy is created with the greatest artistry. She is one of the best juveniles in the SF tradition: tremendously believable, marvelously unstereotyped in a field which likes its female characters predictable. She acts and is acted upon realistically; she is neither a passive heroine nor an invulnerable superwoman. One practically expects her to step out of the page of the book, such is the detail and texture that Gotlieb marshalls to invent her. She is tough, clever, and delightful. What other heroine in science fiction wonders in the midst of her adventures what Margaret Mead would have done?

Gotlieb says of her characters: "I gave Shandy my own personality . . . plus a hell of a lot more brains. Part of Jason's character was meant to commemorate a cousin I was very fond of. . . . Grace Halsey was modelled on a doctor at the University of Toronto Health Service in the mid-forties. . . . She couldn't use her hands and had to have a nurse hold the instrument with which she diagnosed my earache. I only met her once but never forgot her dry humor and radiant smile. During that time I had a friend who visited a home for incurable children, and I went along . . . I kept up acquaintance with one of them for many years, and wished very much that I could give them something valuable. All I could manage was the symbolic gift of the powerful Doydoy." As in real life, the division between Good Guys and Bad Guys is shadowy. Is Curtis Quimper a Good Guy? What about Colonel Prothero?

Even the climax avoids stereotype, though we are not told this until after it has occurred. Shandy, Jason, Prester and Doydoy do not Save The World from the Dumplings. The computer in Chicago is one of four, each capable of taking over the functions of the others. What the Dumplings *do* achieve has no value for them. They don't care about Shandy's newly discovered identity. They have lost Doydoy (to his good, but not to theirs). Their sortie into the world results in their own reimprisonment. Their search for freedom culminates in a renaissance they did not desire and in which they have no part.

Irony intervenes again. At the end of the book Shandy says to Jason, "I'm too different. I thought I'd be with everybody again . . . and now I've just been kicked upstairs and pushed out!" (p. 158). The opening of Sorrel Park will probably make Shandy's life easier and more pleasant. But despite Jason's reassurance, she knows she is going to be—for a while—just as lonely and misfit and out of place as Curtis Quimper is in the library. The self-aware superperson is free—to do what?

The response must be that the superperson is free to do what any and all human beings are free to do within the limits of her abilities and the bounds of moral choice. This is by no means a new message. But *Sunburst* tells it in a sensitive and vital way. Gotlieb's narrative is clear and swift and her characterization is compelling. At a time when popular literature seems to deny the responsibility of the generations for the future and for each other, her unashamed attention to principles is necessary and refreshing. It needs to be preserved.

Elizabeth A. Lynn
San Francisco

REFERENCES

1. All quotes from Phyllis Gotlieb are extracted from personal communication between Gotlieb and Elizabeth A. Lynn in August, 1978.

2. Peter Gellatly, review in *Library Journal* 95:1035, March 15th, 1970.

3. Biographical and bibliographical data obtained with the help of Charles N. Brown and Dr. Susan Wood.

4. *Sunburst,* Fawcett edition, pp. 50–51, 117–119.

Girls and boys, come out to play,
The moon doth shine as bright as day.

Curtis Quimper ran down the midnight street, silently screaming into the minds of all wild things.

LaVonne Hurley, a dwarf with a twisted compressed body and a mind equally ugly, teleported herself into the street and scrambled on short thick legs . . .

Frankie Slippec jumped off the windowsill, floated downward like a balloon, and ran with the rest . . .

Donatus Riordan threshed and screamed in his bed. When his parents ran into the room they found him hovering near the ceiling. Suddenly he disappeared, and there was a queer sucking noise as the air rushed in to fill the space he had occupied . . .

They ran down the main street to the center of town, melting the asphalt in the roadway and burning the clothes right off a sleeping vagrant. They exploded the cans in a grocery store, and a flying fragment hit Billy Phipps in the neck and cut his jugular vein in two. And finally the police came and knocked them out with stunguns.

sunburst

by Phyllis Gotlieb

An Original Gold Medal Book

GOLD MEDAL BOOKS

Fawcett Publications, Inc., Greenwich, Conn.
Member of American Book Publishers Council, Inc.

for Kelly, of course

sunburst: 1

IT WAS Shandy Johnson's thirteenth birthday, and she had celebrated by treating herself to a vanilla cone and a licorice stick. Alternately blackening her tongue with one and whitening it with the other, she was about to step up on the curb at Tenth and Main, when a boy who had been holding up the lamppost on the corner favored her with a long low whistle.

She was startled; first she looked back to see if he meant somebody else. There was no-one there. Then she glanced into the plate-glass window of Fitch's Joint to see if she had turned within the last moment into something rich and strange; she hadn't. She was still a very tall cranelike girl, rather sallow, with narrow torso in a navy sweatshirt and long bluejean legs like articulated stovepipes. A high forehead and pointed chin gave her face the look of a brown egg poised on the small end, and her long crinkly black hair was tied in a ponytail with a shoelace.

She sniffed and rubbed her nose to make sure that it at least was still on the straight and narrow, then took a fast hard look at the young man.

She would have thought he had escaped from the Dump, if that were possible. He had a boxer-crouching bullethead set on a bull neck, thick arms, and a barrel chest tapering into short legs and small feet. But he was so obviously an extreme of his type she began to wonder if he hadn't escaped from a zoo. He had a longlipped chimp mouth, and best of all, one fantastic black eyebrow curling around his eyes and across the bridge of his nose. All he needed was psi.

He gave her an innocent cheerful grin; she replied with a level surly glare and went past him into Fitch's Joint, cramming the stuff in her mouth and wiping her hands on her pants.

"Hey, Fitso, who's the monk on the lamppost?"

Fitch put down the glass he was polishing and leaned over to get the view. He jerked back fast. "Hell, it's the Dumper's peeper!"

5

"Jason Hemmer?" So he did have the psi. She flashed her teeth. "I thought he didn't look kosher."

He regarded her curiously. "How come you didn't know him yourself?"

"I keep out of the way." She admired her black tongue in the mirror. "And I got spies."

Fitch picked up the glass again, but his hands trembled. "You better scram through the back."

"I don't think he wants you, Fitso."

"If he's read you he don't need nothing else. Listen, Shandy"—pursing his rosebud mouth, he rummaged in the cash drawer and tossed her a crumpled bill, —"get on a bus and hole up in the east end."

"Me? I don't need this! Like you say, if he's read me—"

"Shut up!" He snapped his flowered armbands and added through his teeth, "Just get out!"

He turned his back on her and she frowned once at his bald head and wedged the bill in her tight side pocket. She took one more glance through the window. The chimp was beginning to move, and she scudded out the back door without waiting to see if the lamppost fell over.

She threaded her way among garbage cans, ran down the trucking lane, came out on Tenth, and settled into a gentle ostrich-trot. She looked back once, swiftly. Hemmer had not yet come round the corner and was probably still talking to Fitch. He would know where she was, but his psi range was small; she could keep up a strong, if awkward, loping run and lead him by the nose.

Just in time she noticed the blue-uniformed man lounging with crossed legs and folded arms in a doorway between stores. She slowed down casually and walked with eyes straight ahead, but not without observing that he was a big ugly customer. He was a member of the CivilPolice, and if he decided to stop her she was in for real trouble.

Jason Hemmer was working for the Military; they only wanted to know if she had psi, and she didn't. If they caught her she would be measured, psyched, rorschached, and given a Prognostic Index, in itself a safeguard against being put in the Dump. But being pulled in by the civvies meant Juvenile Detention on the top floor of the county jail, a sickening prospect. Civvies played rough, dirty, and for keeps, and she would spend her last breath escaping them.

The CP gave her a suspicious glance as she went by, but it was four o'clock and he had no excuse to ask her why she wasn't in school. Then she remembered Fitch's money in her pocket and broke out in a cold stinging sweat. If he found out about that—!

She was beginning to have the feelings of a desert animal circled by kites and vultures. Like the town of Sorrel Park itself, a patch of carrion land surrounded by barbed wire: on the one hand at the mercy of a martial law that swooped and seized children to be caged in the Dump, and on the other, victimized by a vicious and rapacious Civil Police.

But the CP made no move to stop her. She had run these risks every day of her life, and her luck had held once again. She took a deep breath of relief; she was free to waste her day dodging Jason Hemmer.

The late afternoon sun was slanting as she rose into the lovely mellow light on the rooftop of Pyper's Drygoods, crouching and silent. Douggy Pyper was there, feeding the pigeons; they were cooing and flapping about his thin freckled neck and he did not hear her.

She said in a low voice, "It's Shandy. Jason Hemmer's after me. You want to take a look down?"

He was at least half of the spy system she had so impressed Fitch with. For him, as well as herself, espionage was the natural function of a child in an adult world. He nodded, barely turning, and went over to the parapet, a pigeon still clinging to his shoulders. "Nobody there yet," he announced, and went back to his task.

She was confused. He should have known where she was. She crouched for a few moments in the shadow of the pigeon-cote, then rose and slipped quickly over to the next rooftop, past chimneys, Tri-V aerials, and skylights like great quartz crystals.

After three more stores there was no place to go. She sat down in the dirty corner of the roof, circling her arms round her sharp knees and rubbing knobs of licorice off her teeth with her tongue. Let him come and get her, dirty spy.

Jason Hemmer was the only psi outside the Dump; probably the only free one in the world. The forty-seven psychopaths penned in the Dump possessed more personal powers than had ever been known to mankind; he paid a price for his freedom by scouting the city for new psis as they were born, or more likely, as their powers developed during childhood. No parent could hide a child from Jason Hemmer, and no-one in Sorrel Park considered him a lovable character.

Shandy wriggled in discomfort on bits of gravel and slivered brick. She was sure if she edged her eyes ever so narrowly over the parapet he would be on the sidewalk among the threading people, facing up with his cockeyed grin. I pspy. Her lip curled. *That* for you, she spat at the invisible enemy.

She got up on her knees and poked her head defiantly over the rim, intending to stick her tongue out at him, and pulled back in surprise. He was not yet in the street. Now there was something funny here. He was a telepath, he was homing on her—or was he only playing a trick to scare her on an idle afternoon? But Jason Hemmer was not an idler in the street. He was as anxious to avoid the civilians who despised him for a baby-snatcher as he was to keep out of the way of the CivilPolice, who loathed him as an arm of the martial law.

Her knees were too sensitive to rest on for long, and she picked herself up and looked over the rooftops, but there was no-one in sight but Douggy. Arms akimbo, she surveyed the narrow horizon. It was a dispiriting view, limited by barbed-wire ramparts, reaching into the sky, only in grime and smoke.

Sorrel Park had never made many claims to grace and beauty. A midwestern town on a waterway, supported by grain and, originally, coal, it had grown without planning, and its architecture was Ugly American; but the people were not. At least they had not begun that way.

America's "Open-The-Door-In-Eighty-Four" policy had had a noble sound overseas, and a year of quota-free immigration had swelled Sorrel Park, as well as many other small towns. But ten years later all doors to this place were closed. The explosion of the reactor at the nuclear power plant had brought in the Military to place the town under martial law and suppress the news for fear of countrywide panic. Sorrel Park stopped in mid-growth, left with nothing but the dubious distinction of being the only community in the country on coal power.

The children of its once-hopeful immigrants had not learned the new ways of America, because new ways did not filter through barbed wire, or prosper in an almost nonexistent economy. Outgoing mail was censored, and little of the promised money made its way back to families in Europe. Fifteen thousand men and women who had brought determination and industriousness lost heart, and the place withered and shrank back on itself. A generation had been cheated. With twisted spirits they began to cheat in return.

For Shandy it was what she had always known—but not necessarily home. She accepted and despised it as she accepted and despised the existence of Jason Hemmer, a living symbol of the second great cataclysm that had hit Sorrel Park. Twenty-two years later when the MPs were about to move out, the powers of psi had awakened in the children of parents who had had radiation damage from the Blowup. Jason Hemmer was the luckiest of those children.

Shandy knelt at the roof-edge and looked down into the street again. This time she saw him.

He was trotting round a corner on the opposite side of the street, trying to look unconcerned, and a failure at subterfuge in his new workshirt and clean jeans. He stopped uncertainly, looking this way and that, and people on the sidewalk stepped around him, frowning, but he seemed not to notice them. He crossed the street at a slow run, lumbering, but with a kind of heavy grace, like Neanderthal at his best. She suppressed a flicker of admiration and narrowed her eyes; he fetched up on the sidewalk below her, looked both ways once more, and scratched his head.

Evidently he didn't trust his telepathy; he tapped a passing woman on the shoulder. She blinked at him once, bridled, and recoiled. Then she opened her mouth and began to yell, "I don't know and I don't—" Two or three men ran up as she got a good grip on a big purse and swung her arm back, and Shandy, watching from only a few yards up, bit her knuckles to keep from laughing aloud.

Jason Hemmer had cringed like a boxer warding off a blow. After a frozen moment he relaxed and straightened, and moved quietly back against the wall. The man and the woman, dumbfounded, began looking about wildly. Somehow he seemed to have disappeared from their sight.

"Up to his goddam tricks," one of the men snarled. "Did he hurt you, lady?" But the woman merely sniffed, shook her fist at the empty air, and went her way.

The men melted, and Jason Hemmer moved out, and stood silent on the pavement. Shandy could have spat on his head.

But she no longer wanted to. A cold knot of uneasiness was tightening itself in her belly; she should not have been able to see him once he had decided to disappear. There was something strange going on.

So far, the chase had not been a matter for concern. She

did not want to be caught by the MP but, since she had no psi, she was not afraid of the Dump and once she had taken the battery of tests she would have learned something.

Now she sensed there was more at stake than a game of cat-and-mouse with a little temporary inconvenience at the end of it. Sure of the outcome before, she had been almost eager to match wits with the Dumper's peeper. Now she could wait.

She watched, fascinated, as he shrugged, scuffed his thick shoes on the sidewalk, jammed his hands in his pockets, and shambled down the street.

That was that. He knew where she lived. She would give him plenty of time to go there and stir up a hornet's nest with Ma Slippec. It was some comfort that nobody connected with the MPs was likely to give anybody up to the CPs. She rose and crossed the roofs again, prepared for a serious discussion with Douggy Pyper on the depredations of the pip.

She walked home slowly in the soft evening light; lamps were coming on. She had no intention of holing up in the east end. Fitch was a scared little man and she had better uses for his money.

When she came within a block of Slippec's Cigarstore she knew she had made a mistake. There was a stir about the place with plenty of yelling and screaming. Reason told her to jump on the next bus, but she went ahead; seeing the dark-blue CP uniforms milling around she began to run.

They were dragging a scratching, screeching ragbag out of the store. It was Ma Slippec, a gaunt woman with scraggy black hair, in a torn dress and dirty shawl, and she was thrashing furiously. Her son Karel and her daughter-in-law Rosie were pulling at her from behind, and the civvies knocked their arms down with billies.

"Lemme go, ya sonsabitches!" she bawled. Crack! went the billy on the side of her jaw, and she subsided in howling and gibberish. From far back came the sound of heavy instruments crumpling the still in the backyard bombshelter.

The thermonuclear blowup had crippled freedom long before Shandy was born. The psi explosion had killed it for good when she was too young to grasp all of the implications, and she had never lost her sense of freedom. After a childhood spent dodging the heavy-handed Slippecs, she still had no fear of violence and no idea how to stop it; she ran in blindly angry.

A thick hand closed around her arm and pulled. She twisted, striking out, and found herself facing Jason Hemmer.

"Damn you, you did all this!" She knew this was untrue even as she said it, kicking out in a blind fury. "Let me go!"

"You nut!" He pulled her down the street and into a dark doorway. "Want to get your jaw bust too?"

She whispered, close to tears, "They're hurting her! They're—"

"She'll be back in a week, all wired up. Civvies gotta have their fun."

She shivered. He poked his head out for an instant. "They got her in the wagon. Come on!"

"I got stuff in there, upstairs—" She pulled back. "Clothes and—and books—"

He looked at her. "You wanta go ask them nicely? Never mind, I'll get it for you. Get going!" He yanked her down the street and into a deserted alley. "Now that stuff," he said. "Where?"

He had let her go, and she rubbed her arm, still trembling with outrage. "Read me and see!"

"Go without!"

"All right!" She breathed deeply. "Small back room, upstairs."

He closed his eyes. "Yeah, they got somebody tearing up the mattress."

"Nothing there. Orange crate by the bed: two pairs socks, two nightgowns, pants,"—she reddened in the dark—"jeans, jersey, khaki duffel . . ."

"Okay, busterboy, now you see 'em, now you don't. . . ."

Whuck! The khaki duffel looped its drawstring around his wrist, swinging with weight. He opened the neck: pouf! pouf! Two ragged cotton nightgowns puffed and bloomed in the air above him; he held out the bag and they went in. Pop, pop, two pairs rolled-up socks, pants, etc.

"That all?"

"Yes—gimme!"

"Not yet. I had enough goose chase with you. Come on!" He pushed at her. "Git the lead out. You nearly got us both beat up already."

"Not you," she said bitterly.

"Me? Listen, a guy throws a brick at me, I can keep it off. Two, three, maybe. Ten guys and ten bricks, I get seven bricks." He laughed shortly. "If I could do any better I might be in the Dump instead of helping MPs shove other guys there. You had supper?"

They had stopped in front of Jake's Eat-It-And-Beat-It, and she hesitated. She had been expecting supper at home, but it didn't look as if she'd get it. "No," she said finally. She was hungry enough, though what she had seen back there had taken the edge off her appetite.

As he pushed the door open she said, "Will they serve you?"

"Sure, they'll think I'm a gooky red-haired guy with a big nose and an Adam's apple. You'll see."

She had eaten in plenty of greasy spoons before, including this one, but now the rank stale odors and slopped counters made her long for Fitch, with his crackling clean white shirt and mauve armbands with roses.

They slid into a booth and the potbellied counterman came over, wiping his wet hands on a filthy apron.

"Hiya, Shandy. What's yours, Red?"

"Why don't I?"

"Why don't you what?"

"See you as a gooky red-haired guy with a big nose and an Adam's apple."

He shoveled the last of the pie in his mouth and worked his strong jaws around it like a grazing animal, and was silent.

She said crossly, "All right, keep it a secret. At least tell me what you want me for."

"I don't know."

"You don't know! That's a lie!"

He ignored the insult and said, "I don't decide any of these things. They tell me, 'Jason, go get Blank.' So I get Blank."

She looked hard at him. His brown eyes were lazy and amused. Hunger over, she had begun to be aware of herself again. The booth, built to encourage fast turnover, cramped her ungainly limbs. When she thought she was leading him astray, she had felt perfectly competent and self-assured. Now, under the eye of the enemy, she was all odds and angles, a square out of Flatland, and dirty, sweaty and defeated besides. She tried hard to control her temper, waiting till he had filliped a cigarette out of a pack and stuck it in the corner of his mouth, and then she said. "Please give me back my stuff now."

"Not yet." One eye crimped against the smoke, he bent down and lifted the duffel. "Whatcha got in here, rocks?" He reached in a hand and pulled out a book. "Hah! *The Web and the Rock!*" He flipped open the cover. "Sorrel Park Public Library—no card . . . why were you so anxious to have me get out *this?*"

She said desperately, "If the CPs had found it they could have pulled me in for theft."

"Good enough reason, I guess—but fifteen cents would have got you a card."

"And my name on somebody's register."

He had pulled out an even heavier volume. "My God! *Rorschach's Test, Volume I, Basic Processes* . . . but this must belong to—" he turned up the flyleaf, "—yeah." He looked up and shook his head. "You never went to school."

"No."

"Jeez, I'd hate to have to test you." She giggled. He asked with interest, "How'd you make out with it?"

"Like Huck Finn'd say, it was interesting, but tough. I got through it."

"How'd you get hold of it?"

"He was giving a lecture at the Y—you know, telling them what was being done for the kids? So I snuck it out of his briefcase when he was answering questions. But I haven't touched his notes and markers. Was he mad?"

"Mad!" He snorted. "But how could you get away with it? There was only grownups supposed to be there."

It was her turn to snort. "Listen, when I was six years old I used to carry bottles from Ma Slippec's to Fitch's in a doll carriage four-five times a day. Nobody ever asked me: whatcha got in there, little girl? Nobody ever asked why I wasn't in school, CPs, MPs, truant officers."

He said seriously, "I can understand that."

"I can't. I know I'm bright—what else is different about me besides this?" She indicated her stringbean proportions.

"You sure you're bright, now?" He was grinning.

"Why?"

"Fitch gave you some money."

She hesitated. "Yes. What's that got to do with it?"

"How much?"

"If you don't know, it's none of your business."

"I read him, so I know. Now *you* tell me how much."

She hadn't taken time to examine the bill, and named the highest reasonable figure. "Five."

"No, ma'am. Twenty dollars."

"You're nuts!"

His single brow rose to an even more laughable shape. "Didn't you even look at it?"

Exasperated, she hooked a forefinger in her pocket, dug out the bill, and spread it carefully on a clean spot among the dirty dishes. It was a twenty. She looked at him suspiciously. "Did you have anything to do with this?"

"I haven't any reason to do anything of that kind, Shandy."

She had to take him at his word. "Wow, this is more than all the money I ever had added up together!"

"Why'd he give it to you?"

"What are you talking about?" She drew her dark brows together. "To help me out."

"Kind of sudden, giving you a twenty right away just because you saw me"—his grin broadened—"holding up the lamppost."

Her heart beat faster. "So what?"

"How'd I get to see you, when you'd been practically the invisible girl around here, these thirteen years?"

She got the drift at last. "I don't believe you," she whispered.

"How come your Ma Slippec got picked up by the CPs just two hours later?"

The words rose to her lips: you want to smear everybody with the dirt you deal in. But she knew it wasn't so. She glanced up and saw Jake picking his teeth and watching them impatiently. They were the only customers in the hiatus between supper and after-movie, and he was anxious for them, having eaten, to Beat-It so he could duck out and hoist a couple from a jug of Ma Slippec's corn. He was a dirty man, but not a bad one. Evil in a clean white shirt had just never occurred to her before. Not Fitch.

"So why did he give you the twenty?"

"For a Band-Aid on his conscience."

"Right."

She looked down and played with crumbs. Jason asked suddenly, "He ever dandle you on his knee, or anything like that?"

"No . . . he did clip me on the ear once for busting one of his bottles, but I never held it against him."

"So he's no loss."

He didn't understand that. She had known Fitch for ten years. It was the loss of a ten-year belief that you knew someone very well. "But why would he do a thing like that?"

He drew in deeply on his cigarette. "The government is thinking of opening up Sorrel Park."

She digested this for a moment, but was too tired to care what it might mean to her. "What will they do about the Dump?"

"That's what they haven't figured out yet."

"I haven't heard this around."

"Fitch did. I guess he's got contacts."

I got spies, she had told Fitch. She guessed it had meant more than a kid's game to him.

"Anyway, he's been running a blind pig eight or nine years, and it was okay as long as the Sore was closed up; nobody cared too much. People wanted the stuff, and fancy goods weren't coming in. The police have gone easy on bootlegging and petty crime as long as it didn't reflect on the rest of the state, or the country. People on the outside didn't know about it. But once the Sore is open we gotta clean up. That's why the CPs are busting up the stills."

"And Fitch?"

"Like I say, he's been running a blind pig. He knows he'll have to give it up, but he doesn't want to go to jail over it. He wants to be all ready for a nice fresh start. He figured he'd strike a good bargain with the CPs and the MPs: Ma Slippec to them, you to us. Buttering the bread on both sides."

"But I'm not valuable," said Shandy. "Not from his point of view. I have no psi."

"He said you were different," Jason said. "He didn't know why, but that it might be worth our while to find out."

Shandy picked up the bill and folded it into a wad.

"So you see that money's kind of dirty."

"I never did anything dirty to get it." She shoved the bill down where she hoped to have a cleavage one day, but it only crackled down her washboard chest and lodged in a fold of her jersey.

He had recoiled a little, but he only said quietly, "I wasn't trying to take it away from you . . . what I want to know, Shandy, is—if you're so bright, why didn't you figure Fitch?"

She thought, why is he willing to sit here and talk like this, when it's getting so late? He wouldn't have understood the answer she had for his question: Fitch had been an unemotionally accepted and unquestioned part of her life for ten years. Aside from Ma Slippec she had no-one else, and without him there would be a hiatus in her spirit. "I can't read minds, Jason."

His eyes clouded. "Well, maybe I'll tell you something now. I can't read yours."

She sat very still. "Not at all?"

"No. You're an Impervious."

"Is that—is that what's different about me?" It explained a lot. She felt a wild excitement rising in her.

"Oh, I think Fitch's story was probably hogwash. But this is one genuine thing. If there's anything else," he added cheerfully, "we'll find it out."

Oh, no you won't, Jason Hemmer! My plans have changed!

He picked up the check without looking at it, and dug in his pocket. "You know, you don't realize how hard it is for me to talk to a person I can't read. It's a nice change, though. Talk about change,"—he poked around in his palmful of coins—"I hope we don't have to use that money of yours."

"You can wash dishes!"

He laughed. "You think they really get washed here? Listen,"—he turned serious—"maybe you know now why you managed to stay inconspicuous."

"Fitch greased a few palms, saving me up for now?"

"Ah, now you're getting nasty-minded, and I liked you better the other way. Save the crack! No—Fitch isn't that complicated. Most normal people have latent or vestigal psi. It's a lot stronger in babies and little kids, but it's a kind of clumsy and inarticulate thing and it withers away when better methods of communication develop. But adults can still feel the presence of people they can't see, most of the time unconsciously, or nobody could ever hide. With you it's different. Anybody who notices you has to practically tread on your toes first. I even have to concentrate hard before I can see you in anybody else's mind. You're the first complete Imper I've ever come across. That's why I whistled."

"Is that right!"

"Yeah, that's right." He had that cockeyed grin, now, that she had expected, looking over the parapet. "Grow up a little, Shandy. Maybe I'll whistle again."

"Don't wait for me!" she snapped. As he stood up, still smiling, she said, "I want to go"—she jerked her head—"back there."

He sat down again. "I'll wait for that."

So wait, amuse yourself, read about Rorschach's test. She did not turn her head on the way to the *Ladies,* although she had no intention of seeing or being seen by Jason Hemmer again. With twenty in her pocket she could afford to leave behind the duffel with her ragged possessions. When she was inside with the door closed she transferred the money back to her jeans and reached up on tiptoe to unlatch the tiny frosted window. Nobody but herself could ever have expected to get out by it, and even she had her doubts. The last joker who had painted here, God knew when, had cheerfully slopped the guck over latch and hinges; she had to kneel in the filthy sink and wrench with all her strength to get the thing open. The waft of fresh night air that came in was something the like of which the place had never known.

With one foot on the sink rim and hands supported on the upraised window, now never to be closed in a thousand years, she hooked a leg over the sill. She worked like a contortionist to get the other one over, and inched out writhing on her hard hips. She had to turn her head to get it through, and nearly lost an ear on the sill.

Grimacing with pain, she was about to let go, when she found out why Jason had been so willing to let her sit and talk. It was too late.

Two hard hands clamped on her ankles; a voice in the dark said, "It's okay, Buck; I got her." And she came down into the upreached arms of two tall grinning MPs in tans and armbands (not flowered).

sunburst: 2

MY NAME is Sandra Ruth Johnson. I was born in Sorrel Park on June 3rd, 2011. Both my parents were born here; their families had settled in thirty or forty years before. My father's name was Lars Johnson, and it was his grandfather, Olaf Jensen, who came here from Denmark and changed his name to make it sound more American, though the family still kept giving their kids first names like Nels and Kristin.

My father was a kind of ratty, vital little man with freckles and white eyelashes. He was a steam fitter at the power plant, and he had arthritis badly in his hands. The fingers were hard and callused and permanently curled from handling pipes and wrenches. I think he took drugs for it, but even so he never could lay his hand out flat on a table.

My mother was the big soft type of woman that always seems to marry a little scrawny energetic man. Her name was Katherine O'Brian, and her parents were born in Ireland. She had very black hair and blue eyes. She cleaned offices at the plant while they were running the thermonuclear pile, and after the Blowup, when the old coal plant was put to use again, she went over there until I was born, like most of the other workers who survived, and my father kept on wrenching pipes.

I know that some of the people involved were able to have children soon afterwards, but though my parents had had the injections against r-sickness they hadn't had any kids before, and then they were sterile for about seventeen years, and I guess never expected to have any. And my father had been hit in the back by a piece of hot material, and the wound never quite healed. I imagine my arrival was kind of a surprise. My father was forty-seven when I was born, and my mother forty-two. I think. I was three and a half when they died, and since I can't remember much that happened before I was eighteen months old, that means I can't have really known them for more than two years, so maybe I haven't got everything down correctly.

I couldn't tell you whether they were any different from

other people, or any better. I only know that I loved them. My father used to dance me around the room, singing, "Shandy, Shandy, sugar and candy!" and we played all those games that most very little kids play with their fathers. My mother used to wallop me once in a while, but I never considered this particularly unfair; she wore clean cotton housedresses so full of starch they crackled. Not like Ma Slippec—though there was some kind of queer suffocated goodness in her too.

I remember very clearly the day my father went into the hospital for the last time. I was nearly three and a half by then. After my mother had packed a few things for him she took the dressing off his back and went into the bathroom to make a fresh one so he could start off clean. I had had a popsicle and came in because my hands were sticky. I was supposed to stay out of the way but they were upset and didn't hear me. My father was sitting on the bed with nothing on but his briefs; his back was towards me . . .

She lifted her head and looked out the window, sucking the top of the pen; a small puff of summer cumulus moved blindly across the field of a vision haunted by memory:

A sunburst with twisting rays of exploded scar, and between the rays thick brown keloids; a humped center of ruined flesh, cracked and oozing, ebbing out beyond the cancerous moles into coinsize blueblack naevi, paling and decreasing till they washed into freckles on white skin.

She jerked her mind away, past the man at the desk and the other one watching immobile in the corner, down to the scribbled pages.

. . . heard a noise and turned. His mouth opened wide; he was about to yell at me and then he stopped. He looked terribly shocked for a moment; I don't know what he saw in my face—I'm not quite certain of what I was thinking, but I do know what I saw. He took a good deep breath and said in a much more gentle voice than he had been going to use before, "Run out and play, kid." I went back out and played and after a few minutes he came down with his suitcase and kissed me goodbye. I never saw him again.

We lived over the grocery next door to the Slippecs, and my mother left me with them when she went to the funeral. I didn't do any crying, and I heard Ma Slippec say to Karel, "That kid gives me the shivers."

When my mother came back from the funeral in her black dress with her eyes swollen, she hugged me and cried again and said, "You just don't know what it's all about, do you, sweetie?" But adults don't realize how sensitive even not very bright children are to these things. I've seen it plenty of times in the children of the oldest Slippec boy and girl, and as far as I can tell they're about dull normal.

My mother had stopped work when she had me, but when my father died she had to go back to her old job and she had the Slippecs take care of me. They were a rowdy lot, always having the kind of fights that blow over like summer thunderstorms—but they weren't mean. My mother didn't care much for them, especially because the old man was in jail again as usual, but she figured if Ma Slippec could keep her own six kids alive and healthy she could do the same for me.

But then my mother started coming home more tired and sick every day. First she couldn't get my supper, and after a while she could hardly get me to bed. I began to be afraid. My father had gone away so casually . . .

One day she couldn't go to work, and she stayed in bed for a few days—she was terribly pale, and her skin was hot. Ma Slippec called the ambulance for her, finally, and packed her some clothes in the same suitcase my father took. She smiled at me from the stretcher, and said she'd be back soon —but she'd become thin . . . her hair was so black, and her skin so white against it . . .

Shandy put the pen aside and lined up the sheets, and folded them across, down over her closed childhood. She got up, handed them to the man at the desk, and went over to the window.

Outside she could see a courtyard, surrounded by a brick wall with iron gates. There were three jeeps parked in the court. She had been brought here by one of them the night before. Beyond that there was an asphalt pavement; an electrified fence, sentry-guarded, enclosed all of this and also a huge acreage empty of everything but grasses, wild flowers, and the Dump.

A great circle bounded by a wall of heavy fieldstone covered with concrete, topped by barbed wire, and implanted with several dozens of huge antennas emitting the buzzing scrambler circuit known as the Marczinek Field. It was impossible to see what was inside the Dump, and she did not want to. Sometimes the dull wash of a savage roar of sound beat against the windowpanes. Other times there was only the buzz of the Field.

Beyond the Dump, the vast meadow, and the fence, there was a deep culvert, last ditch against the road threading the world outside.

Urquhart cleared his throat rather peremptorily and she came back to the little table and sat down. He was a youngish balding man with hornrimmed glasses; his elbow was resting firmly on *Rorschach's Test:* he was its owner. He pulled a thread from a frayed cuff and folded his pink rawboned hands. He had made little red-ink notes on the margins of her ms., which she imagined as: *Use of "ratty" in conj. w. father—signif.?* and *Sight of scar—poss. trauma?*

He had not bothered to ask her whether she had read up on Wechsler-Bellevue, Stanford-Binet, Charlebois, Porteus, because Jason Hemmer was useless as a lie detector in her case, and with psi in question no-one took anything on trust; he had been obliged to make do with whatever methods he could devise on the moment. His manner was not bland; she had stripped the tools from his hands and he was not in a mood to forgive her for it.

She herself was beginning to wonder if she had been so smart. It might have been a great deal simpler and safer to take the tests cold and perhaps learn more at the outcome. But she was interested. She had played one round of the game with Jason Hemmer and lost, without resentment; she was ready for the second.

Some crazy chance had decreed that when the psi mutation hit the human race it would choose the type of child most likely to develop the delinquent type of psychopathic personality, and every one of the forty-seven Dumplings had been through Urquhart's mill, psi and all. He could marvel that he was still alive. She felt that dealing with an absolutely non-psi, and an Impervious as well, could be a welcome change of pace for him.

Psi is for psychopath, what I am not, and don't you forget!

Urquhart unplaited his fingers and leaned down to switch on the tape recorder. "You feel justified in labeling the Slippec grandchildren as dull normal?"

She was taken aback, but answered, "As long as I'm not handing out the Prognostic Indexes."

"Do you have any evidence for this kind of judgment?"

"Three years of close observation; I did a lot of baby-sitting."

"What did you observe?" The words might have been assumed sarcasm. The tone betrayed some genuine interest.

"Co-ordination, speech and play-patterns, vocabulary, group interaction,"— she shrugged, —"what you look at in kids."

"Why?"

"I don't know why. I just wanted to know."

"Anything in particular?"

"Only whatever there is to find out."

"That's why you took this—" He thumped the Rorschach with his elbow.

She reddened. "Partly. Mostly I wanted to know how to keep out of the Dump."

"Every child in Sorrel Park has been here—except you, and most of them have gone home again. Why did you think we might want you particularly?"

"I didn't want to take any chances. I admit now that taking it wasn't such a bright idea."

He humphed and built his long fingers into a steeple. "You say here, about your father: 'I don't know what he saw in my face.' I wonder about that."

She waited.

"I think you do, you know. You say what you realized about your mother, when she became sick. I think you might try to remember what you thought when you were looking at your father's back."

She admitted, "Maybe I can, but I don't know that it's not a false memory."

"Why should it be?"

"Because it still doesn't seem reasonable, even to me, that a three-year-old, no matter how bright, could look at that thing and know that a man was going to die from it—and that it could show so clearly in my face he could read it there."

"Why not reasonable *even to you?*"

"Because once you've lived with psi you can accept a lot of other unreasonable things."

Urquhart shifted in his chair, and the man in the corner brought out a pipe and tobacco-pouch.

"Don't you think it's more likely that what shocked your father was your *calm*—after the initial shock of finding you looking at something he normally concealed? The fact that you didn't cry at the sight?"

Shandy said calmly, "The only time I ever cried was when my hands or my body wouldn't work the way I wanted, or I couldn't find out something I wanted to know. I could throw tantrums over those things, but not sorrow or fear."

"Pain?"

She smiled. "Not from being smacked. I went into a rage. if the pain was the result of my own clumsiness."

Urquhart pinched his lower lip and looked at the sheets again.

Shandy folded her hands in her lap and said gently, "Try Rorschach?"

As Urquhart raised his head, glaring, there was a subdued rat-a-tat-tat from the corner, and both turned their heads. The thin old man who had been sitting so silent and immobile was now trying to bite the pipestem to keep from laughing. He had a narrow ascetic hawkface and a thick quiff of white hair. Though he was wearing army trousers, his shirt was a gaudy cotton emblazoned with palm trees and sunsets, a duplicate of which Shandy had seen Mrs. Pyper retailing for $2.49.

Early in the morning, through the window of her room, she had heard a resonant bass voice singing "Many Brave Hearts Are Asleep in the Deep," and when she stuck her head out she saw the bent back of the old man in his colored shirt; he was digging in a small flowerbed beneath the window. He complemented the flowers in his shirt, and his selection of plants was as wayward and eccentric as his taste in clothes. Wild, blowsy poppies straggled in and out madly among ragged tulips with dropping petals, colors crazily mixed. Alternately he hummed, bellowed, or swore as he rubbed a callused thumb. She had wondered what his place was in the scheme of things here.

Urquhart, glancing at him, said, "Come off it, Marsh." His tone was tolerant, almost bantering, and Shandy for the first time looked thoughtfully at the man himself. He was wearing a tweed suit, not tans. Perhaps to emphasize a difference, as the older man had done with the loony shirt. But the latter had succumbed to army pants, while he . . . *I'm only here as a temporary consultant, thank you, so I won't need . . .*

Eight years. He had been a lot younger when he first heard of the strange consequences of the Blowup. A rising young psychiatrist? Some older doctor's Bright Young Man? The suit was frayed. Eight years docked from the prime of learning and earning. Forced as well to learn the techniques for giving and analyzing Rorschach and other tests because it wasn't feasible to keep a whole battery of psychologists and psychiatric social workers for forty-seven children with whom it was almost useless, as well as dangerous, to come into contact.

"Well," the man in the corner broke his silence. "Sheath the swords and call it a draw."

Urquhart smiled. Then he said, "Listen, Shandy, I'll admit I haven't the patience and tolerance I once had and ought to have now. I'm not trying to burn you down to the stump. But I like to find out things about people too."

"But I have no psi."

"You haven't *now*. I know that; even if you had some special or superior kind I don't believe you would have been able to conceal it all these years. But even with your height and age you haven't reached puberty yet—and I've seen how these things work. Who knows what you might be able to do later?"

"Then why—"

"No, I'm not worried about psychopathic or schizophrenic trends. But you are an Impervious. I've never seen one, and I want to know how you tick. It's special and rare, and it might be very useful to us one day." He sighed. "If you weren't so young, it'd be a lot of use to us right now."

But he would not elaborate.

She rested her arms on the sill of her window and looked out into the evening. Her room faced away from the Dump; she was glad of that. There was a stretch of lawn around the flower plot, and beyond that, the brick wall with its gate, the asphalt road, and several wooden barracks buildings for the Military. Lights were on in them. She thought of the lamplight she had watched in the dusty streets the evening before, when she was free.

She had not seen Jason since she arrived. She had sat beside him on the hard jouncing seat of the jeep, grateful that noise and movement had made conversation impossible. She had sensed him becoming glummer and glummer as the ride went on, and finally when they turned into the court-yard and were getting out, he had looked at her, warily, and said, "You mad?" She had said no, and that was it.

There were no bars on her window, but it was two floors up. Unless she were willing to break her neck it was useless to climb out. The room was clean; it contained a bed, table, chest of drawers, and chair. There were a closet and a small windowless bathroom off it. She would have considered it luxurious if there had not been a soldier standing guard outside the door.

She had been interviewed by Urquhart, measured and encephalographed by a white-coated woman doctor in a wheelchair, pumped for minute autobiographical details by a grim Colonel Prothero; she was feeling raw and badly used. Her mind and person, private all her life, had been probed too deeply within the day to suit even her enthusiasm for the acquisition of knowledge.

What am I? I want to know . . . but I won't find out from them . . .

Lights were blinking out in the barracks, and even in the other wing of the redbrick ell she was in. Soldiers slept early, and so did their commanders. Her light was out. She got into bed and slept.

She leaped awake completely disoriented, blinking at the foreign shapes of the cracks of light round the door and the starlit window. She shook her head. There was a racket down below, and the barked commands, doorslams, and running about had brought her a rare nightmare: she had crouched in the street with Jason once more, shivering and sick with the terrors of the CP raid. Now wide awake and listening, she felt a small stab of fear.

Nearly everyone in Sorrel Park shared a contempt that was deep and sincere for both the civvies and the MPs. At the same time they had developed a fear of a Dump escape comparable to fears in other times and places of plague and atomic war. Shandy was aware of the incongruity of these emotions, but she had some share in both of them. Only, she sometimes sensed, to have a bond with humanity . . . because, when she thought about it, she had little to lose.

She ran to the window and looked out. All was calm outside; the grounds were tinged with dull yellow light from the windows below. She opened the door a crack. The soldier was gone, perhaps called down by whatever emergency was going on. She could get out of the building now, probably, but the gates would be manned. And there was excitement going on down below. She headed for it.

The iron staircase was cold to her bare feet; on the lower floor she discovered the source of the noise from the first doorway. The door was ajar.

She pushed it open a little further and peered in. The room

was adjacent to Colonel Prothero's office, and in its opposite doorway two soldiers were supporting a person almost unrecognizable as human. His head was hanging down and his clothes and skin were covered with blood and incredible filth.

She glimpsed Prothero snarling and knuckling his yellow-bristled head as though to pull all the hair out. He was in pajamas. Khaki. The woman doctor, crisp, and immaculately white-coated as she had been during the afternoon, swiveled her chair in front of Shandy's line of vision and said quietly, "Lay him down on the couch there."

The spattered thing hanging between the soldiers raised its head. It was Jason Hemmer. One eye was closed and black; he had a bleeding bruise on the cheek below it, and his lips were swollen. He muttered thickly, "Figured they were asleep . . . they were laying for me . . ."

Prothero snuffed like a horse. "You heard what she said! Get him down there!"

Shandy craned her neck as the men set Jason on the couch. The doctor wheeled over and obscured the view, dabbing with swabs of cotton and antiseptic.

Jason's voice ran thickly, broken by groans as the sting of soap and antiseptic hit the raw. "Jocko broke a collarbone, growing in—ouch, dammit!—all crooked—"

"He's a tough one . . ." the woman murmured, turning momentarily to throw a wad of cotton in a wastebasket, "—don't know if he'll let me—"

"Yeah . . . Doydoy's got an open sore on his neck . . . the Kingfish's got an—"

"Hold still, now. This one will hurt."

"—ugh—abscessed tooth, been drivin' everybody else nuts—in fact he started this whole thing with me—"

"Get it all down, Tapley!" Prothero roared. "What are you gawking for, man?" Tapley fumbled for his notebook.

"—and LaVonne—she's hopeless!"

"Well, you'll try to sort her out for me tomorrow," she said cheerfully. "That's about all for now, isn't it?"

"Yeah. Oh—" Jason raised himself up on an elbow, gasping painfully, and Shandy saw his grimacing face over the white shoulder. "Colonel . . . Colin's all right."

Prothero grunted.

Shandy, unable to restrain herself, had slipped into the room, flat against the wall, in the shadow by the door.

"And Frankie Slippec?" she whispered.

Jason turned his head. "He's okay, he—hey! Who are you?

I never saw you before—jeez, I can't read you! What—"

"Lie back, Jason dear," the doctor said, and added without moving, "and you, Shandy, go back to bed now, please."

Shandy, suddenly conscious of her threadbare nightgown and her bare feet, cringed and slipped out quickly. But she lingered in the hall long enough to see Urquhart move past the doorway and bend over Jason Hemmer.

"Lie still now, Jason. Go to sleep, boy, and we'll start getting rid of those blocks. That's right, close your eyes. Now I'm going to count down from fifteen, and when I get to one . . ."

sunburst: 3

WHEN THE soldier brought the tray next morning, Shandy greeted him with a Pollyanna smile of such sweetness and radiance that it made her innards lurch.

"There's something wrong with the thing," she said.

The soldier, a lantern-jawed ectomorph suffering from hangover, forced his bloodshot eyes open a little and mumbled, "Huh? Whazzat, little girl?"

Shandy, five-seven in her socks, folded her hands in her lap and piped, "Please, sir, there's something wrong with the thing. In there." She jabbed a finger in the direction of the bathroom.

"I don't handle stuff like that, kid. You'll hafta wait'll I can get a plumber."

"Oh, please! I'm sure you can fit it. I just don't know how it works."

He sighed, rubbed a head that was almost visibly throbbing, and shambled toward the bathroom.

"Right in there," she said. She had the chair ready, and once he was inside she slammed the door and rammed the chairback under the knob. She put her mouth against the crack and yelled, "Hey, boychuk, soak your head, you'll feel better!" and was out in the hall with the door closed behind her before the first muffled bellow escaped.

There was no-one in the hall, but that state of affairs wasn't going to last long, and she was anxious to discuss a few things with Jason. She tiptoed down the rattan carpet. Most of the doors were closed and she didn't dare open them; a couple of open ones revealed beds and tables as stark as her own. There were two last doors at the end. If they yielded nothing she would have to go back and face the wrath of her captive, or try her luck downstairs. One room was empty, but from the other a low voice called, "Shandy!"

He was in bed, wearing a pair of white pajamas with blue arrows that gave him, with his close-cropped head, the look of a Dartmoor convict. His face was black and blue, but most of the swelling had gone down. She wondered if he were able to use his psi on himself.

"Hi." His look was still wary.

"Hi," she said cheerfully. She struck an exaggerated pose against the doorjamb and said with deadpan insolence, "You look like you forgot to ask yourself what would Margaret Mead have done."

He half rose from the bed, and she was about to run, but he lay back and said, "Never mind. Maybe I'll ask you that one day."

She grinned and sat down on a chair by the bed. Jason folded his arms in back of his head, looked up at the ceiling, and said casually, "You know, somebody's just busted outa the can, and whooee, is he mad!"

At that moment there was a yell of outrage from down the hall, and Shandy was out of her chair and behind the door with the swiftness of reflex. Her eyes were on Jason, but not to beg. He could do as he pleased.

The voice roared through the doorway, "Hey peeper, you see where that—that goddam brat went?"

Jason let it hang for a fraction of a second. Then he said quietly, "Why—she's in her room, Davey. Where'd you think she could get to?"

"Gee . . . yeah, I guess you're right . . . but I sure thought there was somethin' funny goin' on for a minute."

She waited till the steps had gone down the hall and sat on the chair again. "Psi's handy."

"I get some use out of it once in a while." He reached under his pillow and found a crumpled pack of cigarettes.

She indicated his beaten face. "I thought you were only a talent scout. I—I didn't realize you had another job."

"I don't advertise." He shrugged irritably. "Somebody's gotta find out what they need to have fixed. Did you think we just left them to rot in the Dump?"

"But you take all these risks—and they hate you in Sorrel Park. If they knew about this—"

"When they see me they don't usually want to stop and give me a chance to explain."

"You could make them know."

"So what?" He blew smoke at the ceiling. "They figure they know all they need to know about me. They know I can read their minds and make them do what I want. They know I can pick off their kids and get them put in the Dump. Isn't that enough?"

"They might understand."

"No. Not the kind of people that have that kind of kids. It might give them a snide laugh to know their kids can beat me up once in a while. Maybe I shouldn't deny them that bit of pleasure—but it's not a good pleasure, so it won't hurt them to miss it."

She looked down at her hands. "It gave me no pleasure. And I used to despise you too."

"You're different."

"I hope so." She looked out of the window at the barbed wire, the brick wall, the iron gates. "Why are you doing all this?"

He sighed and blew ashes over the bedclothes. "Nothing stops you."

She stood up. "Maybe I don't know enough about dealing with people. I'll keep out of your way till I do."

"Sit down, you silly nut. I told you it's hard for me to talk to anybody I can't read."

She sat down unwillingly. He said, "Somebody's coming, don't get scared."

She waited. Jason ground out his cigarette and said, "Marsh."

"It's me." The old man came in. He had exchanged the orange and green sunsets for red tropical flowers with blue leaves. "I came to see how you were. I see you already have company."

"I'm ready for the next trip," said Jason, with only the faintest hint of sarcasm. "Shandy, this is Dr. Jaroslav Marczinek."

"Oh," said Shandy. "The Field. Now I know why you're here."

Jason sighed again. "You'll never get a simple good-morning from this girl."

"Good morning, Dr. Marczinek," said Shandy. "Why were you sitting in with Dr. Urquhart?"

The old man ignored Jason's snort, but sat down and began to fill his pipe before answering. "Because, since I find it impossible to grow outward in these confined circumstances, I have to do the best I can to grow inward." He clamped the pipe in his teeth and calipered his skull with both forefingers.

Shandy nodded and turned to Jason. "It's nothing to be peeved at. Other people ask you questions when they come here."

"I know ways of shutting them up," said Jason. "With you it's different. And the people who ask you questions have a reasonable purpose."

"I am different. How do you know I haven't a purpose? Just because *I* don't know what it is doesn't mean there may not be one hidden inside me . . . Dr. Marczinek, you seem to find me very amusing."

The old man finished out his laugh. "Oh, yes indeed, and very refreshing—though you may also turn out to be very dangerous."

"And you're awfully truthful."

"You mean awesomely, I hope. I have to be—"

"Now Marsh—" Jason began.

"I can see why you have to be hypnotized," said Shandy to Jason.

"What? You're way ahead of me—"

"When you go in to check on the Dump. Urquhart sets up the blocks so they won't know everything that's going on."

"That's right."

"Do they ever try to break the blocks?"

"Not usually. They might make it if they tried hard, but it's too much like work. Luckily most of them live on the surface."

"And the rest?"

"I dunno . . . there's one or two . . . never mind." He touched his bruised head experimentally "If the toughest ones were really smart . . . and the smart ones really knew how to use their power and their brains . . ."

Marczinek said, "Jason, before I forget, Grace wants to know if you're feeling well enough to complete her lists of broken teeth and dislocated shoulders."

"Yeah. Tell her to come along. You met the doctor, didn't you?" he asked Shandy.

"Yes," said Shandy. "How does she take care of the kids?"

There was a bit of an edge to Jason's voice. "She wheels herself in there and cleans them up, and they treat *her* very respectful and polite."

"How come?"

Jason grinned. "I let them know Prothero told me he'd drop a bomb on the Dump if they so much as gave her a cross-eyed look."

"But he's not gonna drop any bombs for you."

"Nope. You don't have to mention anything about bombs

to her, though. She's a nice old doll without a mean thought in her head, and I don't want her feelings hurt."

"He's a man of true sensibility," said Marczinek. He had been puffing at his pipe and watching Shandy with a curiosity as unabashed as her own. "Shandy, you were saying before that you felt different. Why?"

"I don't know why . . . I've just had the idea since I was very small. I've been trying to find out something about it ever since."

"You are Impervious, solitary, inconspicuous. Along with intelligence, I should think that would be enough. Everyone is different."

"Everyone is individual," said Shandy firmly, "but nearly everyone is a lot like hundreds of other people. The kids in the Dump are a lot like each other—and like plenty of others who aren't in the Dump—except that these are extremes, and they have psi.

"But I'm not like most kids who get brought up any old way; that's part of it. I haven't had much love or attention spent on me for the past ten years, but I've never wanted to break out against everything or hate the world for my tough luck. I'm not unhappy." She shrugged. "Sometimes I think I must have something missing, and sometimes I think I have something added on, and if I didn't have it I *would* be unhappy. . . ."

"A kind of equilibrium," Marczinek suggested.

"I guess so. Something like that. But I see other people who I'm almost sure haven't got it, and they seem to get along all right, even with their ups and downs . . . and sometimes I get frightened. Not the way I'd be if I had psi: if I had a tremendous power I couldn't understand I'd get really scared. It doesn't bother the Dumplings—they've got no imagination and all they can see is that they have something they could get even with, and it must drive them nearly crazy not to be free to use it. You're lucky to have a use for it, Jason, even if you do get banged up."

"Why are you frightened?"

"Because . . . once I read a story about a man who had the feeling there was something special about him . . . he was going to have some great and maybe terribly dangerous part in shaping the world. He loved a woman who wanted to marry him, but he was scared because he figured he was going to be called on any day to save the human race or lead the Charge of the Light Brigade, and he didn't want to leave her widowed—"

Jason exploded. "Jeez, what a jerk!"

"Yeah, he was, because when his life was over and she had died he realized the only thing special about him was that feeling of being special, and he had missed everything that would have made his life valuable or happy. And that's why I get scared."

Marczinek puffed in silence for a moment, and said, "I don't imagine you're the type to turn down a good thing when it's offered to you, Shandy, or refuse to go after it once you see it clear."

"I hope not," said Shandy. "Maybe I'm only being silly."

"No," said Jason somberly. "I thought I was different once, too."

"But you had more to go on than I have. How did you find out?"

"Like you read about in stories. I was about ten . . . out playing alleys with a couple of guys named Charley and Pink. I had a winning streak all of a sudden—I guess I must've been wishing extra hard because I didn't have many alleys—and Charley knocked my best purey out of the ring and said: beat that, you jerk! And I said, 'You're damn right I will!' and they both looked at me as if I was nuts. Charley says, 'What did you go say that for? I never said nothing to you!' And I started scratching my head . . .

"It was funny, you know, because I could still hear the echo of my own voice in my ears, but nothing before that. I says, 'Didn't you say: beat that, you jerk?' He turned white as a sheet—he's Iroquois, and it took some doing—and said, *'That's what I was thinking!'*

"Jeez, was I scared! I shoved my alleys in the bag and ran for home, up the stairs and sat on the bed, just shaking. My mother was running the mixer down in the kitchen and hardly noticed I was there. I didn't want to talk to *anybody*. I was grabbing that bag of alleys so hard my hand hurt, thinking: I start out with sixteen alleys, now I've got fifty-seven—and I've read a guy's mind . . . like that stuff in stories, and maybe I really could do something with my mind. So I put the alley bag on the floor and loosened the string and said, 'Git outa there! Git outa there!' Nothing happened, and I didn't know whether to be disappointed or glad. I thought, well, I'll try once more. I willed them to come out and squeezed at them from my whole insides, and wow! there was a rumble in the bag and they started to pour out and rattle all over the floor.

"Rattle! It was thunder! You'da thought the Imp bust outa the bottle. If I was scared before—it still hurts to think of it. They were shooting out so hard I had the idea they were going to bounce off the walls and ceiling and beat down on me like hail. I scrunched down in the bed and closed my eyes. My mother yelled up, 'Jason, what's all that racket!' and I couldn't say a word. When I got the nerve to open my eyes they were on the floor, just a few of them rolling around a bit. I grabbed them up and stuck them in the bag and that was it."

"And you didn't play again for a while, I suppose," Marczinek said.

"Well, no, I didn't have that much imagination. I was too scared to try anything else for a. day or two, but I was working myself up to it. It was too important just to forget. But I didn't see Charley and Pink around—I think they must have spread the word and everybody was leaving me alone—but I didn't care much because I wanted to work it out. I mooched around like that for a couple of days . . . worried my mother because I wasn't coming home crudded up with dirt from head to foot. And one night when I went to bed I swore I was going to try it out first thing in the morning . . ."

> Girls and boys, come out to play,
> The moon doth shine as bright as day;

The moon was shining. Shandy Johnson, a sallow, thin child of five, slept in the narrow cot. Her sleep was silent and still and almost dreamless; she was not disturbed through the night, even though two or three of the Slippec girls were tossing and muttering in the big bed across the room.

It was a quarter after eleven. Sorrel Park was a small city; there were not many people on the streets on an early September evening. The place was quiet, though there had been rumblings of uneasiness in the last few days. Several fruitstalls had been turned over; no-one saw who had done it. Three manhole covers had disappeared; neither they nor the thief had been found. A bottle had exploded in the hands of a drunk as he was raising it to his mouth; it took two internes three hours to pick the glass out of his face and hands—he had only just missed losing his eyes. The thimble-rigger at Muley's Inn had lost his shirt and his self-confidence.

Jason Hemmer had won too many marbles.

There were ripening talents in the place, scattered, raw, and destructive. They belonged to children who gradually, over months and years, had singly awakened to an unchildish power and begun to use it in bursts of destruction. They were self-centered, out for the advantage. The only minds they were interested in reading were those of a fellow crap-shooter or a beaten-down mother from whom they might bully an extra dollar.

Twisting restlessly in sleep, flying and powerful in their dreams, they were unintegrated, waiting for a form: twenty-nine-boys, five girls, sullen, discontented, hostile.

One other ten-year-old boy besides Jason Hemmer was deeply disturbed. He was lying awake, furious because his father had whipped him for stealing a jet-scooter and staying out after dark to avoid punishment. His name was Colin Prothero; his father, the Major, was fifty-four years old, too old to remember what a boy was like. The boy had careered about the dark streets, swift and free, until he was caught by the CivilPolice, an added indignity for the Military. He lay still in his bed, rigid with anger and resentment.

His parents were asleep in the next room. They could sleep; it was nothing for them to shame him. He tightened his closed lids, squeezing furious red stars of hate against his retinas. And heard voices. A voice.

Dammit, why should he turn out like? He's had every. I always. When I was his. And it had to be the civvies. Why?

His father was awake, then. So much the better. Let him suffer too. He waited for his mother's answering murmur. The house was perfectly silent. He heard his father turning in bed. Silence. And again: *In the morning, see about . . .* and a mind sunk in sleep. A mind—not a voice drifting into the unconscious. *A mind.*

A talent stirred. Almost unaware of what he was doing he began to probe—down into that goddam thick skull of his father's, under the khaki-bristled hair, under the cortical laminations of sternness, resolution, duty—and stopped, repelled by a pain he could not understand.

He retreated, frightened at the enormity of the sudden power, and twitched nervously on the bed. The pain of his welted back washed over him and woke the anger once more;

he forgot everything else. *When I grow up*—when he grew up, what then? What could he show that unyielding man? He didn't dare plan revenge, but he could catalogue the crimes of injustice and humiliation against him.

Someone whispered in his ear: me too.

Who?

Me, me, me, me, me too.

Thoughts flickered in and out of his mind like dust-motes in a sunbeam. The beam thickened and whitened: sleepers were stirring in their dreams, awakening thoughts caught in the pulsing flow. It grew in the mind, a white singing like blood in the compressed veins of the brain. Old men twisted in tangled nightclothes, caught dreaming in passions withered through seventy years; babies woke shrieking as though their brains had been seared in the lightning of mindforce.

Touched off by Colin Prothero's pain and resentment, thirty-four minds coalesced in a critical mass, and at last, a discovered form.

Leave your supper, and leave your sleep,
And come with your playfellows into the street.

Curtis Quimper, who at eighteen had known something of his powers for several years, ran down the midnight street silently screaming into the minds of all wild things. He had stolen three manhole covers, and a few nights ago in the dark of an open field had sent them whirling in a planetary dance of hate around his head, clashing like cymbals, at last crashing together in a single welded mass and plunging down through the earth, atomizing moles in their burrows and melting streams of ore in the crevices of rocks below.

I can do that with anything or anybody, anything or anybody, anything or anybody!

If the form was a pack, Curtis Quimper was the leader.

Scooter King, fourteen and six months out of Juvenile Detention, rose at the imperious call. He had been asleep on a pile of sacking in Koerner-the-Florist's woodshed. His father was in jail, and his mother, with seven other children, had almost forgotten he existed. The rotted door shrieked off its hinges and fell at his frantic push; he scrambled out and ran.

LaVonne Hurley, a dwarf with a twisted compressed body

and a mind equally ugly teleported herself into the street and scrambled on short thick legs. Her arm ached terribly because a sister had wrenched it the day before, but she was perfectly happy for the first time in her life.

Frankie Slippec pulled himself out of bed from between his two sleeping brothers, jumped into his pants, and yanked an old jersey over his head. It was full of holes, and his skin shone through them like dull silver coins in the moonlight as he jumped off the windowsill, landed lightly two stories down, and ran with the rest.

Come with a whoop, come with a call,
Come with a good will or not at all.

Donatus Riordan threshed and screamed in his bed. He was a hunchback with *spina bifida* and the children called him Doydoy because of his painful stutter. He had a comfortable bed in a clean room; he was well loved and cared for; his parents were perfectly decent people and there was nothing wrong with his moral sense—but either the Blowup or some other freak chance had done something terrible to the chromosome pattern that formed him and he could not help himself.

When his parents ran into the room they found him hovering near the ceiling; he was yelling and flailing his arms; the sheets were twisted round his useless legs and trailing in a rope. He wrenched them away with the sweep of a powerful arm and disappeared before they could even think of reaching for him. There was a queer sucking noise as the air rushed in to fill in the space he had occupied.

The force flared and streamed; the town was dreaming. Every ugly thought locked in the mind broke free and dragged with it the animal hates and terrors of childhood, the horrors of the Blowup, and all the small bestiaries accumulated by even the sanest mind living the calmest life.

No-one else ran down into the street, though all felt for an instant the flash of the irrational urge. But none of them wanted to go to sleep again, once wakened. They sat on the edges of their beds, trembling, and lit cigarettes, or got up to turn on lights and put on coffee, with an ear tuned for the coming of thunder.

Jason Hemmer stood on the sidewalk, rubbing his eyes.

The telepathic surge had washed him out of his bed and into the street before he was half-awake. He had used a power he had not known he possessed. Behind him he heard his mother closing down the windows against the expected storm without knowing he was out of the house. He stepped into the middle of the road, dazed; the sky was clear with moonlight. Far down, far away, he heard the clamor of the Pack.

They had passed with the sound of Djinns, and their unearthly echo rang in his brain. He could have joined them yet, but somehow he did not, and only stood there, with his arms limp at his sides, looking down the road.

He heard his mother calling in sudden terror: "Jason! Jason!" and he turned back to the house, stumbling on bare feet. He had missed the express to Transylvania.

Shandy slept.

Up the ladder and down the wall,
A half-penny roll will serve us all.
You find milk and I'll find flour,
And we'll have a pudding in half an hour!

The Pack ran down the main street toward the town's center at the crossing. They had no name for themselves, but they were a single entity, and, except for the oddments, very much of a piece. The older ones had powerful shoulders, but they were all wiry and strong, the girls stringy. Their narrow faces tapered like the muzzles of wolves, shapes that marked patterns on the graphs of sociologists, along with the poverty, the hate, the heritage of crime and drunkenness, and the turbulence of movement that for once was dedicated to a single purpose.

Where do we start?

Start at the middle and work out. That's nice and tidy.

Civvies'll be comin' in a minute.

Ya scared mumsyboy? Hide under the bed. Hey fellas, lookit Doydoy! Hey Doydoy, flap your wings!

Jeez, I can't fly. How come he can?

Who cares? Here—take a look around, you guys! You'll never see it like this again!

Beinwinder's Emporium: one, two, three, four, five, six, seven, eight plate-glass windows . . . bye-bye!

Now melt it, Scooter—hey, you missed one! Yeah . . . now make the fire green and blue . . .

I never knew you were artistical, Buttsy.

Vogeler's Antique-y Shoppy—yeah, yeah—let's stick old Vogeler in there first—"Gitcher filthy mitts offa that stuff!"

Never mind him—wow!

Here, Nolan's Marketeria . . . them cans'll pop if y' git'm hot . . . that's it, boy!

Who's that?

Sergeant Fox?

"Hel-lo, Foxy, ain't this a beeyootiful quiet evening? Hey, Foxy-loxy, don't touch the gun, you'll burn your hand!"

Gee whiz, he done it. Ain't he a nut? Look Ma, no hand!

Noisy, isn't he?

"You broke my wrist bringin' me in, Foxy, remember?"

Too damn noisy. Shut him up, LaVonne.

There's the sirens. Th' civvies're comin, hooray, hooray!

Okey-doke, LaVonne, just goo up the road a little.

"I'll stop their noise, too," said LaVonne. "I like things quiet."

sunburst: 4

"I SAW IT ALL—I heard it all." Jason Hemmer twitched and sweated in his bed. "I went in the house and crawled in bed, told my mother I'd been sleepwalking, and she didn't ask any more questions. My God!" He shivered. "I was lying there—and I knew everything—and I wanted to be with them. I had to be with them!"

"Why weren't you?" asked Shandy.

"It'd be terrific if I could say I was too moral . . . but I think I just wasn't strong enough—not to do all the things they were doing. And I hadn't the hate gathering up in me all those years . . . ordinary kids are full of fight and fury but they don't usually grow a cancer out of it."

"Doydoy?"

"He was scared—and he had too many powers for them to dare let him go. He doesn't really belong with the rest."

"He shouldn't be in the Dump, in that case."

"What would you do with him, Shandy? He's one of the strongest as as far as psi goes."

"Mmm—and LaVonne?"

"Ugh!" Jason grimaced. "Listen, nobody's ever claimed the Dump was the perfect, or even a decent, solution." He lit another cigarette. "So I was lying there, watching it all like a movie, scared to death and wanting to be with them at the same time—and the police came up. At least they managed to run up on the sidewalks when the cars were bogging down in melted asphalt. The MP was on its way, too, by then. The kids were waiting. They'd already found Old Foggy sleeping in a doorway and burned his clothes off, and they had some dinky plans for the civvies—oh boy!— but just as they were about to start the fun one of those burst cans popping out of the store hit a kid in the neck— it was Billy Phipps—sliced the jugular and killed him. When they saw their own blood, they stopped."

"I'd have thought they'd be tougher than that," said Shandy.

"Not then. The extent of their power at the beginning

depended on the Pack's being at full strength. When one of them died they weakened and separated. Gee . . . a lot of them were kids my own age . . . a couple of girls in night-gowns and braids . . . all scrunched together and scared to death. Doydoy was trying to crawl away on his hands . . ." He swabbed his head with a corner of the sheet and it came away wet.

"You knew him?"

"Yeah. I used to call him names when I saw him wheeling around the corner for a bottle of milk and a pound of tomatoes."

"You were only a little kid then, though."

"Yeah. I know. I—I tried to get him away . . . I knew he wasn't one of them, and even if I wanted to be with them I knew it wasn't the kind of thing I ought to want."

"But that's just where Urquhart would separate the sheep from the goats, I bet."

"Sure—I was a sheep then and I'm a sheep now. I had a very low pk range, not in their class at all. But I'm glad I tried.

"Anyhow, the civvies came up with stunguns and knocked them over. Then they carted them off to the morgue and laid them out like logs, all unconscious, and tried to figure out what had hit Sorrel Park. That was twelve-ten a.m. The whole damn thing took less than an hour, and the middle of town looked like a baby A-bomb hit it.

"Prothero took over right away—of course, he had Colin in the thing, too. He dragged out all the doctors in Sorrel Park, got them cleaning up Foggy and Sergeant Fox—and boy, they were a mess—and got Washington on the phone, all within two hours after the bust."

"He looks like the type," said Shandy.

"Yeah, but he's not stupid, and he'd had plenty of experience with emergencies after the Blowup. This place has been a top-secret-emergency deal for a long time."

Marczinek added, "Sorrel Park hardly belonged to the Union after twenty-two years of isolation. With the whole country on nuclear power the news of a serious accident, rare as it was, might have turned everything awry."

"I can't believe it was right to hide it," said Shandy.

"I won't argue, my dear, but the suppression was supremely efficient. I had only the vaguest recollection of the trouble when I was called upon to come here."

"When was that?"

"The day after it happened. I was testifying before a sub-committee investigating un-American activities when the summons came. It was only a few steps down the hall. However," he sighed, "I occasionally regret being trusted so quickly and extensively with classified information. I am afraid my friends must believe I have been wantonly suppressed by the government—and my enemies that I have gone over to the Chinese."

"You didn't have to come, though. They didn't force you?"

"No, I must do them justice. They gave not the slightest hint of force. They begged."

"Why'd they pick you?"

"At that time I was fairly prominent in the field of quantum electrodynamics."

Jason laughed. "Prominent in the field! He shared a Nobel Prize with Brahmagupta for a Unified Field Theory!"

"I see," said Shandy, and continued to watch Marczinek.

Jason slapped his thigh. "She doesn't even know what a Nobel Prize is!"

"I know what a Nobel Prize is," said Shandy.

Marczinek said softly, "Brahmagupta died of cancer of the liver at thirty-five . . . I was with him to the end, and it was a foul death. I am seventy-two years old and I have eleven grandchildren. I haven't seen them for eight years, and one or two of them not at all, but I have them.

"Well. I was sent for. I was told only that it was an emergency, and that if I accepted I must stay until the problem was solved. Now," —he knocked his pipe on his heel— "I know everything and I am too dangerous, like everyone else here . . ." His face was bleak. "I am not strong enough to go through with the brainwash the soldiers here are given when their terms end—and too old to want to lose an hour's worth of memories, even . . .

"Oh, I remember how I first saw them when I arrived here . . . lying on their cots in the hospital, sleeping children. Deeply drugged children. Urquhart and Grace Halsey had taken encephalograms—perhaps you know that they still have the brainwaves of children even today."

"Yes, but their type has a kind of burnout in the thirties, don't they?" Shandy asked. "I've heard their brainwaves change then too."

"True," said Marczinek dryly, "but that prospect at that time was twenty-five years in the future, and we had to do something immediately.

"I had to work from nothing, you understand. Who knows the mechanics of psychokinesis and teleportation? No-one, yet. But there must be some kind of wave between telepathic sender and receiver, the object moved and the mover, the teleport and his destination."

"And you built the Field to scramble them."

"In the simplest terms, yes. I still hardly know what I am scrambling, but the Field covers a wide range."

"Is there a way to break through it?"

Marczinek hesitated. "Theoretically, yet. A bare possibility. Not a thing I'm free to discuss."

"Oh, I don't want to know your secrets," Shandy said hastily.

"Ho, ho," said Jason. "Anyway, it's like breaking into Fort Knox, and I'm the only other person who knows about it. I'm not sure I understand it, so I guess it's safe."

"I can see why you needed those blocks of Urquhart's," said Shandy. "Do you have brainwaves like a little kid?"

Jason grinned. "That's also classified information!"

She said thoughtfully, "Suppose I were in the Dump and decided to make a good deep hole and tp myself up to the surface at an angle, from under the Field?"

Marczinek shook his head. "The Field's a long narrow torus, shaped like a drinking-straw. It goes down into the eternal fires, and up beyond the limits of the atmosphere."

"I'll have to think of something else, then."

"You're not in the Dump yet, so don't worry," Jason retorted. "But you ought to think up something better than that trick you played with the bathroom window at Jake's."

She was sheepish. "That was embarrassing, but I haven't had much experience with psi."

"It wasn't even psi, it was radio!"

"Well, I do a lot better dodging civvies. Dr. Marczinek, how long did it take you to build the Field?"

"Build! They wanted to give me three days to *invent* it! Three days." He clucked resignedly. "To invent a toroidal white-noise field that would scramble everything but light radiations—because growing children need light, even if their souls are dark . . . but it took a week. An old man; a tired brain without the elasticity of youth . . . and I had no Brahmagupta." He began to fill his pipe. "Out in the world it has some use as a cosmic-ray shield for interplanetary vehicles . . . it hasn't my name on it . . ."

"It will," said Jason.

"I think . . . I care less about that every year. It's a pleasure of growing old. Now—on the eighth day we began to build, using components from the old power plant. In the morgue and in the labs we set up here we had a microcosm within the microcosm of Sorrel Park. And confusion. Citizens descended on us in fury, parents screaming: Not my Joey! Not my Frankie! Not my—no, I wouldn't want to go through that again.

"We showed them. We had Old Foggy with second- and third- degree burns over fifty percent of skin area, and he died, eventually, without ever becoming lucid. Sergeant Fox —LaVonne shut him up for good, and he hasn't spoken since." He waved his pipe. "The rage and fury we still have with us. But we simply, could, not, let those children go.

"So we worked quickly. The first Dump was a prefab barracks surrounded by barbed wire immersed in the Field. It was escape-proof even then. We laid them out in there with supplies of food and clothing and allowed them to waken. We felt they might be weak enough to be tractable. It was two weeks after the event by that time.

"We had Sorrel Park at our heels and we wanted them to know what we were up against, so we let them watch. Only adults."

"I saw it," said Jason painfully.

"It was not really a sight even for adults. Those children were growing stronger instead of weaker. They couldn't hurt anyone outside, but in two hours they reduced the installation to charred beams and twisted bedsprings.

"At least after that Sorrel Park began to understand. Our supplies of prefabs and bedsprings were limited, so Urquhart decided to use the classic method for subduing juvenile psychopaths. He left them alone in the mess. Luckily, it was a warm September. When they were crying from hunger we gave them a little food. When they cried for more, we gave them a little more . . . some of them were crying for their mothers. . . . When it became too hard to sleep on the bare ground and they begged for beds, we told them we would give them whatever was necessary—but they must swear not to harm whoever went in to give it to them. And they swore, for what their honor is worth . . . and that is roughly how it has been for eight years."

Jason touched a bruised cheekbone. "Except sometimes they forget."

Shandy said, "It's odd: when you think of psi it looks

so terrific, but when you think of the types that have it—"

"Yeah," said Jason, "but you better not let Prothero—ow!" He clapped a hand over his mouth.

"What—"

"Let my mind wander, dammit! Ouch, it's too late now!"

He was right. Three sharp steps brought Prothero into the room. He was as extreme a mesomorph as Jason, and his shoulders filled the doorway. A clashing red complexion sometimes comes with ginger hair, and Prothero was in full clash.

"Why is that girl out of her room? Who's on duty here? Davey!"

Jason sighed, but his voice was calm and steady. "She's not unguarded, sir. Marsh and I have been keeping tab on her, and besides, she isn't trying to get away. Don't blame Davey. I bamboozled him."

"He shouldn't have allowed himself to be bamboozled," Prothero said coldly.

"It's all right, Steve," said Marczinek gently. "I was only telling Shandy all about the horrors of the Dump, so she'll be good." He clicked his tongue, realizing suddenly that he had said the wrong thing, and Jason muttered under his breath. It seemed to Shandy that it would be impossible to find a right thing to say to Prothero.

But he only grunted, pulled out a khaki handkerchief and swabbed the back of his neck. The skin there was red and crosshatched; it puckered under his touch. He was very nearly an old man. He sat on the bed and put his hand on Jason's shoulder. "How are you, boy?"

"I'm okay, thank you, sir."

"Who was responsible for the brannigan last night?"

"The Kingfish started it, but most of the others chimed in."

"Anybody try to stop it?"

"Not much anybody can do when a lot of them get together on a thing."

"Any change in the status quo?"

"I think the Kingfish'll try taking over from Quimper, soon. They're spoiling for a fight."

"I'll stop that." He rubbed his hard jaw. The fingers rasped faintly over microscopic stubble. He stood up to go, adding harshly, "Have to have a talk with somebody from in there."

Marczinek said, "Steve, sit down a minute." He took a deep breath. "Jason, will you please tell Colonel Prothero—

and me too—honestly and unequivocally whether Colin had anything to do with this mess?"

"No," said Jason immediately. "He did join in after a while when most of the others were in it, but he wasn't anywhere near starting it."

Prothero said wearily, "All right, I believe you. Just don't be so damn careful about sparing my feelings next time— only there won't be a next time." He turned to Shandy. "Now. What do I do about you?"

"I only wanted to find things out, sir. Why I'm here . . ."

He blinked and rubbed eyes reddened with sleeplessness. "Yeh. I guess that's not the worst thing in the world. Urquhart says an Imper's the kind of talent we need to help control the Dump, but don't ask me how he expects to do it." He stood up. "And why I'm here, in the big garbage heap . . . thirty years . . . a nice new shiny lieutenant playing a game of blues-and-grays around the power plant. Then bang! blooey! and we had real blood and real dead men to play with. Broke out geiger counters and dickey-suits, and yanked volunteers out of the county jail." He pointed out the window where antennas glittered under the morning sun. "Those volunteers were their fathers. And they're dead. General Kirsch too . . . Colonel Paterson.

"We cleaned it up, whoever was left of us; we got over the r-sickness. All I could think of afterwards was, thank God! thank God we're still alive. Yeah, thank God."

He turned on his heel and went out, and they heard him bellowing down the hall, "Davey!"

Shandy hissed. "Jason! You're not going to let him chew out the poor guy for nothing! Quick! Do something!"

Yawning, Jason stretched out under the covers and folded his arms in back of his head. "Something for who?"

"Davey, you nut!"

Oh," he yawned again, "I already done that. I knocked off his hangover."

sunburst: 5

URQUHART RATTLED papers on his desk and glanced across at Shandy, who was staring out of the window. They were in his office after a supper she had shared with him and the others in a small dining-room. "What's the matter, Shandy? Why so moody? You're not cooped up in your room any more, and I thought you'd be happy about it."

"I'm still not free." She kept looking out at the soft evening sky. "Do we have to go through all that stuff again, like yesterday?"

"Nope. Different stuff every day. Are you scared I'm going to ask you searching questions about the bootlegging business?" She hunched her shoulders. "Ah, Shandy, you think we'd pull them in and lay charges on the strength of what you'd say? We're not civvies here!"

She turned back to him with a set face. "They were all I had for ten years . . . you didn't get anything new from me."

"No, and I didn't want anything of that kind from you. It's not my business."

"What do you want, then?" she whispered.

"Your mainspring, Shandy! Only the shape of your living spirit. And you're sitting there all shriveled up looking like an old maid who's just discovered the Oedipus complex."

She smiled in spite of herself. "I haven't got one."

"How old did you say you were when your parents died—about three and a half? From what you seem to have remembered up to that time I'd say you had a fully developed personality by then, so I wouldn't count on your not having one. But it's something everybody has, like a navel, nothing to worry about. Trust me. The tape recorder's off; nobody will know your private business."

"Jason knows everything," she said.

"Does it matter?" He took off his glasses and whirled them by one earpiece. "I imagine Jason has his secrets too . . . and if I know anything that shouldn't be told I'm not telling it. To you or anyone else. All right, I know you weren't asking!" He grinned. "Are you the same person I was talking

to yesterday? I could have cheerfully wrung your neck then.
Not the picture of a good psychiatrist. Now I've calmed
down and you're flaring up. Why?"

"I was playing a game yesterday."

"Then why have you stopped playing?"

She looked out the window again. The sky was dark, and
noise rose from the Dump, a wilderness of sound. "I have
some of the same feelings they do. If there's bars around you,
you feel you have a right to try to squeeze through them,
and if there's guards in front of you, you have to outwit
them. Doesn't matter how much people feel they have a right
to put you there. From your point of view they have no right
at all. Ever.

"I saw Ma Slippec beaten up. And you dragged me here.
It didn't seem to me there was much choice between you and
the civvies. But last night, Jason—and he doesn't have to be
here. I and the rest of Sorrel Park are stuck, but he could
use psi and get out. And he's here." She faced his intent eyes
again. "You came of your own will, and Marczinek too.
You've all suffered for it: you, Marczinek, Prothero—nobody's been able to duck it. And the reason and shape of it
underneath the surface is something I've got to learn yet."

"That's the only reason?"

"I'm interested in my future! My guess is you want the
Dumplings handled by somebody they can't use psi on, who
can't read their minds either—kind of a supplement for
Jason. It's what you wanted me for, isn't it? So maybe they'd
get to trust me, and so on? But I'll tell you it doesn't sound
like a workable idea to me."

"It was the general intention, though," said Urquhart.

"Okey-doke. It's kind of a scary idea, but let's forget that
for the minute. I'll even forget you aren't giving me much
choice."

"It's magnanimous of you."

"But if the Sore's going to be opened up you need help
right now, not four or five years from now. And you said
I'm too young. If I'm no use soon, when you need help so
badly, will you keep me on indefinitely and train me?"

Urquhart put his glasses back on and folded his arms. "No.
We'll have to let you go, then."

"That's what I thought! And look what you're doing:
you're trying to scrape me down to the raw. It hurts me to
see Jason beat up, Dr. Marczinek with his family outside,
Prothero . . . and then you have to know what makes me

tick—and I like talking to you, I never had anybody to talk to. I used to get all my emotions from books, and I never thought I had any of my own, so nothing bothered me.

"If I stay around here for a couple of months and then go out there again I'll be a fish out of water and get picked up by the civvies and end up in Juvenile Detention scrubbing floors with some scruffy old bag yelling in my ear and waving a billy around my head."

Gnawing his lip, Urquhart twirled his chair round once, and said finally, "Shandy . . . we don't have sinecures around this place. But we care—for everybody, in the Dump or out. I can't make fancy promises, but I can say that much . . . and Shandy," he added gently, "you've only been here two days and the armor's crumbling. It seems your ideas of what you are and what you ought to be are tremendously different from what you really are . . . don't you want to find out?"

"Yes." She snuffled and rubbed a hand under her nose.

"Then you'd better throw away the armor. You don't want to keep up your membership in the Bootleggers' Association; it's not a going concern. Have you decided what you're going to do when you grow up?"

"Get out of Sorrel Park."

He smiled. "That's all right to start with."

"After that it depends on what kind of person I turn out to be."

"I think you've a much better chance to find that out now. But don't be afraid of being vulnerable. Out there"—he nodded toward the window—"nobody's been able to hurt them—to reach the deep center of their emotions . . . and look where they are."

Next morning, savoring her limited freedom, she found the library. The small booklined room was as uncomfortable as the rest of the building. Two-thirds of its shelves were stuffed with discards from public and lending libraries, donated for the edification of the military and cringing in faded covers with titles as flat as stale beer. The remaining third had been brought in by Urquhart, Marczinek, and Grace Halsey. She could have continued her study of *Rorschach's Test,* but instead she pulled down books indiscriminately.

She skimmed and leafed quickly, sitting on a hard chair (there was no other kind), heels on rung, elbows on thighs, head on hands, as intently as she had exercised her intellectual suction pump for years on illegally borrowed books at midnight in the small back room above the cigarstore: about Jimmy Valentine, Burstad's first landing on Mars, a day at the seashore spent by a dreadfully sweet little girl named Honeybunch, a Welsh town by Milk Wood, complicated abdominal operations beginning invariably with a midsection down the midline, distant nebulae, the ragged men waiting for Godot—and Jason stuck his head through the doorway and yelled that it was time for lunch.

After lunch she picked up Klinghoffer's *Chemical Psychotherapy,* hefted it thoughtfully, and put it down; she had caught sight of Urquhart's collection on criminal anthropology.

She plowed in, skipping tables of statistically significant percentages, and slowly began to build up a picture of Delinquent X, the bad boy in the street.

X was occasionally a girl, but much more often a boy; growing out from crowded and dirty tenements, though at odd times he came from surprising places and ended up in tenements. A father drunk or decamped, a mother more careless than evil; hampered more by dislike of education than by lack of intelligence. A muscular, tapering, rough-cast body, strong and vital, the ideal of the artist and the girl in the street—it belonged to a boy who was restless, irritable, childish: he seriously intended to be a mountaineer, space-pilot, bullfighter when he grew up—if he could do it without hard work. He ran with birds of a feather, and more gracefully than the gangling bookish boy or the cheerful fatso. He wanted things on the minute, and was ready to take them, regardless of what got broken or who got hurt when he did it: served them right, because everybody was against him anyway. But he was going to be something big: maybe a hero, maybe a gangster.

But this was not his future; not to be the giant of crime and destruction—a different breed—but the miserable inadequate, the petty criminal shuffling in and out of court and jail with his record hung round his neck like an albatross.

Shandy put the books aside and rested cheekbones on knuckles. There was something missing in the picture: X had no face. She thought of the groups she had seen over the years at Jake's and Fitch's Joint and all the other joints. The back-room types were usually hurried and furtive working-men, but there were also clumps of kids who worked off the evening on a cup of coffee and a dollar in the jukebox, eyeing the back door enviously. They were noisy, sometimes scuffling, wore fantastic clothes and had plenty of greasy hair growing way down the neck—but their faces were blurs. That was natural, because they were all so much alike; but that told her nothing about the Dumplings.

There were two good ways of finding out what she wanted to know. One was to go into the Dump, an idea she rejected out of hand; the other was to get a look at the Dump files . . . and the Dump files were in Prothero's office.

Ha.

Colonel Prothero, I'd like to see the Dump files, please.

Certainly, dear. Just pull out the drawer marked D.

She giggled. It was a delightful picture. Well, she could ask Urquhart, or Jason . . . but even if they approved she suspected they would want Prothero to approve as well.

. . . But if she went in quietly and inconspicuously, and took them . . .

At supper she was mooning out the window, vaguely conscious of the pleasure of being able to see grass and flowers while she ate.

"For the third time, Shandy," Urquhart said, "will you please pass the butter?"

"What—oh, I'm sorry."

"What were you reading today that's made you so absent-minded?"

"All sorts of stuff—but I was thinking about humors."

"Hm?"

"You know, the old idea that your character depended on what type of liquid you had most of in your body: blood, bile, or phlegm. And you turned out sanguine-humored, or choleric or phlegmatic. Or else it depended on which planet was in the ascendant when you were born, and that made you saturnine or jovial or mercurial. I don't know if the two systems were supposed to work in the same person at once."

"What are you applying them to?"

"Well, you're using the work of Sheldon, the Gluecks, Kaplanski, Cosgrove and the rest to classify every kid in Sorrel Park by body types: endomorph, mesomorph, ecto-morph, or mixtures. That's saying their characters depend on whether they're mostly fat, muscular, or skinny, and—"

"Hold on, you're going too fast. Personality and tempera-ment may depend to some extent on body types, but nobody said anything about character. Endomorphs are fat and love food and affection; mesomorphs are muscular and vigorous—

and sometimes pushy; ectomorphs are lanky and have a sensitivity that might have something to do with the relationship between skin surface and body mass. Those categories are extremes, of course, and though his shape might add to the factors developing a person's character, no type has an edge on brains or morals."

"Well, however you put it, it all sounds like astrology sometimes."

"Not when you find that almost eighty percent of the kids in the Dump are almost pure mesomorph. If we put every mesomorph in the country in reform school it would be silly—and dangerous. But if you measure all the kids in reform school and find eighty percent are mesomorphs, it's not."

"But kids in reform school are *not* eighty percent mesomorph. Only a big enough percentage to set people thinking."

Urquhart smiled. "You're right. I got off the deep end there. But here in Sorrel Park we've skimmed off the cream" —the cream jug rose from the table and set itself into Jason's hand without a ripple—"or rather, the psi skimmed it for us . . . well, if we ever get to open this place up, it ought to be a hive of scientific interest—but I don't think I'm going to hang around and watch it buzz." He turned to Prothero. "When are you leaving, Steve?"

Prothero gulped a mouthful of cake. "Tomorrow." He tossed down his last half-cup of coffee. "Excuse me. Got some things to do first." He pushed back his chair and left.

"Where's he going?" Shandy asked.

"Washington, by helicopter," said Jason.

She looked at their glum faces. "What's the matter?"

"He's going to talk about the Grand Opening."

Urquhart added, "We've got a few private doubts about whether the world and Sorrel Park are ready for each other."

"You mean, about the Dump?"

"Partly. But is Sorrel Park ready to go back on thermonuclear power? For thirty years we've been the only place in the country operating a power plant on coal. Is the world ready to learn what can happen when a thermonuclear plant blows up? What about municipal government? Sorrel Park's been hidden for thirty years, and has the laws and morals of a frontier town of a hundred and fifty years back. Also, there're seventy-five lawsuits against the plant sitting in the books waiting for the day when they can get to federal court—most of the plaintiffs are dead—think of sorting out the descendants! And this isn't counting the Dump, the publicity, and the foofaraw in every country in the world."

"But Prothero seems—"

"Oh yeah,"—they brushed themselves off and stood up—"he's for it, all right. It's his baby."

It put a different complexion on things. She was repelled by the idea of going after the files while Prothero was away. He had trusted her enough to allow her the run of the place. If she took them and were caught it would be bad enough with Prothero here; but if he were away, and some officious lieutenant had a report ready for him—not that she was afraid of Prothero, but . . . It looked as if she would have to ask him. If she were going to be useful there were things she had to know, and she might as well learn them honestly.

Jason walked down the hall with her. "What have you got planned for this evening—more reading?"

"I don't know," she said guiltily. It was on the tip of her tongue to ask if he thought Prothero would let her look at the files. And it was becoming harder and harder to visualize Prothero letting a kid mess around in his file-drawers. And Jason would laugh at her. Don't be afraid of being vulnerable, Urquhart had said. Sure, but she'd seen him when he wasn't too keen on being vulnerable.

Jason was looking at her closely. She was able to read his mind for once: he was wishing he could read hers. "You up to michief?"

"N-no . . . no mischief." She noticed his clothes for the first time. "What are you doing in uniform?" He was very much of a young Prothero in tans.

"I'm in the army," he said. "I'm of age . . . but I've always worn it since I've been here."

"How long?"

"Four years." He grinned. "Those crazy shirts are all right for Marczinek. He could wear a monkey-suit and still look like a professor."

She looked down at her long narrow shape and said wistfully, "I'd like to wear dresses, but I don't think they'd look any better on me than this stuff."

"You'll just have to put on some years, Shandy. . . . I'm going to visit my folks now."

"I didn't know you had any."

"My parents and a sister . . ." He seemed a little embarrassed, as if, having given up all other privacies, he wanted to keep one intact. She would never ask how or if he managed to protect his family from his own stigma—but she wondered.

"Well," he said, "so long," and disappeared. Now he would be outside the barbed wire . . . and home. She sighed and wandered down along the hall.

She stopped at Prothero's office, heart quickening. The door was open, no-one was inside. She slipped in. The door was open as well to the other small room where she had seen the men bringing Jason. Both rooms were accessible to the hall, but the office also led to the outside, and a waft of sweet evening air blew in through the screendoor.

She looked around, and for the first time felt guilty at being where she shouldn't. Desk, chairs, hatrack with army cap—and filing cabinets. Here was the perfect opportunity; but she screwed up her courage, sat down on a chair, and crushed her hands together in her lap. She was almost too scared to laugh at the consciousness of her own nobility.

Then she heard murmuring and footsteps; clattering and the crunch of wheels on gravel. Prothero's voice called, "All right! In here!"

Her nerve failed her in an instant. She turned wildly toward the doorway, but there were noises in the hall too. She dashed into the next room; there was a dark figure at the door. Someone had taken up a post there. She crouched down and squeezed into a shadow beside the couch. Prothero turned on the light in his office, and she got a good look at what the men were wheeling into the room.

It was a cage of heavy wire mesh, so swathed in knobs, rods, wires, dials, antennas and aerials that it was almost opaque. But there was something huddled inside it.

"I don't need you now," Prothero told the men. He moved into the doorway. There was an unlit cigar in his mouth. Fire flamed between his hands and he bent to suck it, his face scarlet in the light, but expressionless. He pulled a chair over near the cage and straddled it, resting his arms on the back, and waiting.

After a few moments the cage creaked and stirred, and the thing inside it sat up and stretched. It was a boy, as undistinguishable as the X Shandy had found in the books. He was no older than Jason: his fair hair was thick and wild, pushed back rather than combed; his face was smudged with dirt. There was a light beard growing on his chin, or perhaps only more dirt. Prothero did not look at him; he sat there puffing at the cigar.

The boy folded his arms around his knees and said with perfect good humor, "Hell, Pop, you didn't have to use the stungun on me. You know I'm a good boy."

Without turning his head Prothero said, "Stand up!"

The good humor faded and the boy stood up sullenly. Shandy saw that he was dressed in the classic prisoner-of-war uniform: a gray coverall with a red target on the chest. Here it must have been worn with a sense of irony; no bullet would hit an escaped Dumpling.

"What do you want?" said Colin Prothero. He added, "I'm not a mind-reader," and grinned; the cage was evidently a small Field.

"Aah, you know," said Prothero wearily. Perhaps he had been through this a thousand times before. He reached back to knock a block of ash into a tray and turned to the boy again.

Colin twined his fingers in the mesh. "You know I didn't have anything to do with that brannigan over your peeper."

"I know," said Prothero. He turned the cigar in his fingers and watched the red flaming through layers of gray.

"You always said I never had enough guts anyway."

"I didn't say that."

"You thought it."

"You should have kept out of my mind, then . . . and proved to me—"

Colin sneered. "What? That I had enough guts to jump Jason Hemmer?"

"No . . . just that you were a person. Not especially a hero—just a human being. With the psi or not."

"I don't know what you mean."

"You know what I mean. You've had eighteen years to prove you're a person. You didn't start the row. You didn't join in right away. And you didn't try to stop it."

"You nuts? You figure I'm gonna help him?"

Prothero looked at him levelly. "No," he sighed. "Maybe I *would* have respected you more if you did start it. I don't know."

The boy laughed. "Great! Now I'm a slob because I *didn't* do anything dirty. If I'd started it you'd have pulled my ears off, eh? Look!" He pounded his fist against the mesh and the cage trembled. "Look, Pop! I'm not scared of you!

You're scared of me, or you wouldn't have me here in a cage—"

Prothero snapped: "You're in a cage because you're an animal! . . . You're in this room because you're my son. I know about Quimper and the Kingfish—but a toothache's no excuse for them to turn you all into wild bulls with *banderillas* in your backs . . . I know them. They think they've got plans to fight it out. It's not going to happen— and I'll deal with them separately." His voice changed and shaded almost imperceptibly. "I brought you here because I hope . . . I want—"

Colin screamed, clutching the wires with both hands, "I don't care what you want! You want! You want me to snivel and cry and lick your boots and be your little soldier-boy! You can go to hell! I want to be out of here, back there! I'd rather die in the Dump than live in the same world with you!"

Shandy writhed in her corner of shadow. She had grown more uncomfortable by the second, and now she was wishing with all her heart that she had braved Prothero's initial fury and made an escape. She glanced toward the door, but the guard had not moved. Perhaps he had grown used to this.

Prothero had stood up. He took the chair by its back and threw it against the wall. The cigar rolled on the floor, scattering ash and streaming thinly with smoke.

"I'll break you!" he whispered. "I'll break you!"

Colin laughed.

"Tapley! Get this thing out of here!"

He turned away as the cage was wheeled out, until it began to crunch on the gravel. He righted the chair, slowly. Under his hand it shook in its loosened joints. He picked up the cigar, set it in his cheekpouch, and absently scuffed at a burned spot on the floor.

He swung into the dark room, snapped the light on, and went over to the sink. His eyes were blank, almost blind. He opened the mirrored door and took out a bottle of branded whiskey and a glass. Then he turned and saw her.

sunburst: 6

"YOU!" He put back the bottle and glass and dumped the cigar in the sink. She stood up. As the cabinet door swung to she glimpsed the reflection of her face, slate eyes livid against dark skin.

"You sneak!" He grabbed her shoulders and began to shake her. Ridiculously she was reminded of Ma Slippec beating her carpets out of the window. "You filthy gutter-snipe! Spying—"

She twisted in his grasp. "I didn't come to spy! I—"

"—sticking your nose in—"

"—came to ask—"

"—everything, digging up dirt! What do you want here?"

"—if I could see the Dump files!"

"There's no money in this place! Human garbage, wrecked lives—"

"I don't want to pry into your life, and I don't want money!" She wrenched her shoulders away from his hands. "I came to ask to see the Dump files,"—she stamped her foot—"to ask, to ask, to ask!"

They stood glaring at each other, both winded. She gulped and finished lamely, "I was sitting here waiting and when I heard everybody coming I got scared and hid."

He said slowly, "Maybe you don't belong in the Dump . . . but you do belong out there in a court of civil law." He took a deep breath. "I don't want you here, but I haven't got all the say in the matter."

He strode into the office and over to the filing-cabinet, jerked open a drawer—her eyes were too blurred to see whether it was marked D—and yanked out a thick wad of folders. He slammed it on the desk and leafed through it with trembling hands, pulled out one folder and threw it back in the drawer. He looked up and said through his teeth, "Urquhart said if you *asked* I was to give you the Dump files." He picked them up and shoved them at her, and she clutched them to her chest.

"Urquhart has lots of bright ideas," said Prothero. "But

57

if you want to know what *I* think, I think he's a fool—and you're a thief! Now get out!"

At the door she tripped, twisted to keep hold of the files, and sat down hard on the hall floor. She saw that what she had tripped over was a foot, and looked up at the soldier by the door. It was Davey. She scrambled up and glared at him, but his face was expressionless.

"Touché!" she snarled, and made her way down the hall, into the first dark doorway, where she found a chair, set the files on the floor, and burst into tears.

Simultaneously the lights went on and the peculiar tp sound broke on the air.

Jason was sitting at the desk. They were in Urquhart's office.

"Auditioning for the next Passion Play?" His voice was heavy with sarcasm. She looked up through the tears and saw her hair had broken loose and was bursting out all around her head. Still sobbing, she reached down, fumbled the lace out of a shoe, and tied it back.

"You nut! You had him all ready to like and trust you, and you had to louse it up. What are you blubbering for?"

"I'm insulted."

He began to laugh.

"Go ahead, if you can get fun out of my pratfalls."

"I didn't think that was funny. Are you hurt?"

"Only when you laugh."

He did his best to smooth his face. "I'm not laughing. Why are you insulted?"

"Because I went in there to—"

"Yeah, I know. You went in there to *ask*. Well, why'n hell didn't you?"

"I got scared."

He snorted. "Oh boy, the Reckless Roamer of Sorrel Park. Never scared in your life . . . so what? So he would've been mad. He wouldn't have bit your head off—just an ear or two. Now look what you did to him. Was he broadcasting! Nearly took *my* head off."

"Why didn't you stop him? You could've."

"Stop him! You're a panic. He's got a head like a bull. I couldn't try anything on him without his finding out sooner or later, and I couldn't stay around here ten minutes after he did. He doesn't really believe it can be done, and I wouldn't want to be the one to prove it to him. All that stuff with Colin—that was his pride being broken for the hundredth time—twice over because you saw it."

She took a wad of tissues from Urquhart's desk and swabbed her face. "I didn't want to see it."

"I know you didn't. But you were sneaky, and you can't be sneaky around psi even if you're an Imper—it's not the best policy. Besides, you heard him. Urquhart told him to let you have the files if you asked."

"Why didn't Urquhart just give them to me?"

"He wanted you to think it up for yourself."

"Oh yeah. So I thought it up and this is what I get for it."

"You got the files."

"I don't want them now—oh, I guess I do. Why did Urquhart want me to ask for them?"

"Ask him."

She rested her chin on her hands and thought for a moment. "Suppose it was like a test?"

He was silent.

"If I'm not interested in people I'm useless—and if I'm too scared to handle them properly it doesn't matter how interested I am. If you look at it that way I've passed one part of it and failed the other." She smiled. "Maybe I've passed a third part by figuring it all out for myself."

He whistled a bar of melody elaborate with grace notes and arpeggios. "Maybe. Figure you know everything now?"

"No. I still don't know why you're here."

His brow became a pair of joined circumflexes, but he relaxed and stretched. "Look in my file."

"It wouldn't be here. These are Dump files."

"Kiddo . . . we're all in the Dump."

She picked up the heap of files and leafed them. Names flicked before her eyes: COOK, Elizabeth (Lexy); DOLLARD, John (Jocko); . . . HALSEY, Grace; HEMMER, Jason; HURLEY, LaVonne; KING, Harvey (Scooter) (Kingfish); . . . PROTHERO, Colin Adams; PROTHERO, Stephen Decatur . . .

She stopped. "Swift said it was a brave man that first ate an oyster . . . Prothero's put his file in my hands."

"Oh, he's brave, all right. But in this case he's just dumb."

"I know he took one out. I guess it was mine. But Urquhart's here, I see. He must have handled the interviews. Who did his?"

"He handed in his analyst's report."

She put the files down. "Does your file tell why you're here, Jason? Don't ask me to look at it. It'll tell me all about when you were born, and what you weighed, and whether you were a good-natured kid, and if you broke windows or stole apples. I don't need that kind of junk. I know I'm the only person you can't read, and you could say it's a good enough reason not to trust me . . . maybe you forget to look at the outsides of people once in a while, because you're so busy with the inside. But you know what people look like and how they sound when they're telling lies; you haven't forgotten everything you learned before you found you had psi."

Jason sighed. "Yeah. It's possible. But maybe you'd like to tell *me* something: why you want to know."

"I want to know why I ought to stay here," said Shandy. "I think I could get out if I really tried. You could say it's my duty to stay, but what do I know about this kind of duty? I'm thirteen years old.

"Nobody knew about you when the Dump was set up. You came here four years later, so you must have come of your own free will. I can see you've got a necessary job, but it's a terribly ugly and dangerous one. Marczinek and the rest just fell into their jobs when they didn't know they were going to have to stay so long. Nobody forced them to come in the first place, but they had age and experience to help them decide. How could you make such a complicated moral decision at the age of fourteen? Why should I even have to think about it at my age?"

"Maybe," said Jason, "we just oughta say that if I couldn't, I'd be in the Dump—and if you couldn't, you wouldn't be Shandy Johnson." He stood up and went over to the window. There was a Walpurgis-Night glow over the rim of the Dump; it gave the watcher the sense of a place where hideous sacrifices were being offered. "That might be nearly all of the answer for you . . . but it isn't all of it for me . . ."

Shandy said, "If you think I'm being too snoopy I won't pester you any more."

"That's kind of an ambitious statement! Nah, I have to be a lot snoopier—in meaner ways. What I'm getting round to telling you, Shandy, is: there's two other psis like me in Sorrel Park."

"Is that right! I guess I don't know them."

"No. I hope you never will. One's a girl—a married woman now—about twenty-four, and the other's a boy of eleven."

"Are they bright?"

He turned away from the window, grinning. "I could've guessed you'd ask that. Bright enough."

"Gee, if they could get along like that, without anybody knowing, maybe Doydoy—"

"No." He sighed. "Not with the present set-up."

"Powerful?".

"Not in Doydoy's class, though the boy's a firecracker. He's strong and healthy and lively, everything Doydoy should have been . . . I never forgot him crawling on his hands like that. I wouldn't let it happen again. I knew Prothero needed somebody like me, because pulling in all the kids in Sorrel Park for examination every year or two was too chancy and sloppy. I got together with the others and worked it out. The kid's too young and irresponsible. The girl would've come, but she wasn't really strong, physically, and she'd been going to get married . . . and I'm a tough lunk and don't look too bright. So I let myself get pulled in. That way I got to have a say about who comes— and who stays. That's all there is." He came over and sat down again.

"You're lucky you didn't get thrown in the Dump."

"It wasn't easy—I had to come out like a solid citizen on the tests, and still not look like I was here on purpose. It nearly got queered because Urquhart figured there was something up right away. But he knew a good thing when he saw it."

"Does he know about the others?"

"He's met them, and he's tested them too. When I was sure I could trust him I thought that'd be the best way to get him to trust me . . . you saw he knows how to keep his mouth shut."

"I can do the same." She bit her lip. "One more thing. I know I really shouldn't ask—"

"Don't let that stop you."

"You've gone through a lot to keep others out of the Dump . . . but you knew I had no psi—and you knew pretty well that if you brought me here I'd be staying. How come you brought me in, Jason?"

He laughed. "It's what I like about your questions: you can always answer with a simple yes or no. Well, kiddo,"— he slapped the desk and stood up— "the minute I saw you, I says: Jason, here's one you don't have to worry about. This doll can take care of herself."

Shandy was sitting on her bed, trying to put her thoughts in order. She was a little ashamed that she had chivvied Jason into telling her about the other psis, but at least she had penetrated the mystery she had sensed around him. She was resolving to leave him alone and try to forget them, when she felt a sudden stab of jealousy. From his words about them she had deduced a network of friendship and dependence among the three of them; the Dumpling pack had evolved nothing comparable.

But she had never belonged to anything, and she didn't belong to anything now, either. She muttered, "Feelin' real sorry for yourself, kook?"

She had just been given her first emotional hotfoot. She had told Urquhart that she had previously gotten her emotions from books, and it was true. Yet, she had also seen the Slippecs in orgies of fury and drunken hate, and had moved aside in her mind to watch them, believing that there was something artificial about them because she herself had never been touched. She conceded now that she might possibly have been mistaken.

If the Slippecs flung their emotions about it did not necessarily mean that they were not real and painful, if only for the short time they lasted. She deduced this because she was feeling real and painful. She had flubbed the business of the files from A to Z and would have given quite a lot to have missed the interchange between Colin and Prothero. She had seen Prothero with something on his back that was every bit as terrible as her father's scar; and the face of X had come too close for comfort. It was not the kind of experience she thirsted for.

Besides all of which she had been chewed out by both Prothero and Jason. She was furious at herself. She trudged into the bathroom to clean her teeth and confronted her reflection.

"Dumbhead!" She snarled at the dark face the locked-in gene of some forgotten Italian or Spaniard had given her, the child of fair-skinned northern parents. Her eyes were red-rimmed.

Prothero had called her a thief.

But she had seriously considered stealing the files when they were hers for the asking all along. She had never thought of herself as immoral—only a person who had to know things and made sure she found out. For years she had toted jugs of corn from the Slippecs' still to Fitch's

Joint, without stopping to wonder whether it was wrong. Prohibition was a stupid business; but although the civvies may have encouraged spying and betrayals, the law did not require them. If the law had been obeyed as it stood would the people have been harmed by it?

The spirit of Sorrel Park had been warped by tragedy, barbed wire, and terribly repressive policing. Did this give the citizens an inalienable right to break laws in order to make themselves sick with rotgut? And she had taken full jugs from Ma Slippec and handed them to Fitch; empties from Fitch to be filled by Ma Slippec.

If she had refused would they have forced her to go on, or found her some other way to be useful? She had never put the matter to a test and now it was too late.

But I was only a kid then, I didn't know what I was doing. And I'm still a kid, anyway. I can't help . . .

. . . thinking like a Dumpling

She tugged at the frayed lace binding her hair. It snapped, and she flung it away. She made a face in the mirror. Beautiful. Now your hair's hangin' down like spaniel ears. She yanked at it, but it stayed. It would have been pretty silly if it had come out.

She noticed a pimple under the angle of her jaw: a stigma of adolescence. That and two hairs in the left armpit. Whee, I'm growing up! She peered down the neck of her jersey. Nothing dangerous there yet. Her feet came to her attention. Long red sneakers, 7½ AAAA, no laces. She kicked the unlaced shoe off her foot into the bedroom and followed it in. Thin soles, rubber parting from the uppers, toes about to come out. They had stained her socks many a time in the winter slush, and no new ones in sight. *Mebbe when I git the new batch out, dearie? Couple jugs oughta make it?* Even if the cigarstore had not been a front it would not have brought in enough money to buy her shoes. Her life had been founded on immorality.

There was a pair of new white shoelaces on the bed. She smiled at them; she was grateful, but it was a pity Jason couldn't have managed the shoes to go with them. She threaded in the new laces, pulled the heap of files onto her lap, and immersed herself in less personal problems.

Q: Do you know what's happening now?
A: You got me hyp—hypma—
Q: I've used drugs and hypnosis to inhibit your tp and pk.

You may not understand my words, but you can still read my mind and you know I don't mean you any harm.

A: Yeah . . . I guess . . .

Q: And it's no use trying to fight. You're much too sleepy. You've got quite a record with the civvies, haven't you, John?

A: Call me Jocko.

Q: All right, Jocko. I was talking to your mother and father and—

A: That ain't my pop. He's in the bughouse. That's Moe.

Q: Moe? Moe who?

A: I dunno. Moe, shmoe. Who cares?

A: Stephen Decatur . . . yeah, my people had me slated for the Navy—but I ended up in the Army instead—sure, they were upset . . . I've always had a funny feeling that I got into all this trouble because I went against them—don't tell me that's irrational, I know it already.

Q: I don't tell people they're irrational—I just try to help them figure it out for themselves.

A: Well, I figured it out for myself, but I'm no further ahead.

Q: That hasn't gone far enough as an insight. Maybe you could get some help out of a couple of years of analysis.

A: Analysis! Lie around on a couch and tell some clot how I wet the bed when I was eight years old!

Q: Did you? How old were you when you stopped?

A: None of your goddam business!

Q: There's something I can't figure out here, Jason. Your file says you were pulled into juvenile court when you were nine years old for malicious mischief—you and Charley Longhouse threw some rocks into Koerner-the-Florist's window.

A: Yeah, that old bat. The judge gave me probation—my father didn't, though.

Q: Then you apparently went straight, did well in school, and kept off the books altogether till the day before yesterday, when you broke into Chremsler's Market Garden and started teeping cabbages and potatoes down Alicia St., giving Mayor Hough a black eye in the process. If it hadn't been for that, nobody'd have known you were a psi. How come?

A: Well, gee, I guess I just kinda went crazy, that's all.

Q: That so? Um, tell me, Jason . . . do you like having psi?

A: Not much.

Q: Why not? You can get what you want, read people's minds—

A: There's not much to take around here, and I got my folks here, so I don't want to leave . . . the insides of people's minds isn't something you want to live with every day, some people, anyway. Things get spoiled: I see a nice-lookin' doll comin' down the street all dressed up, and she's thinkin', *Is the powder covering the pimple on my nose?* Oh, you can laugh. I'm only fourteen, I got plenty of time—but I don't see why I hafta get my ideas all squashed before I'm old enough to really enjoy 'em. It's no ball having psi.

Q: Maybe not—but I wouldn't mind knowing what you're thinking right now.

A: Honest, Doc—nothin' there but the ordinary junk.

Q: I think I'd like to be able to judge that for myself!

A: Help!

Q: I'm trying to help you, son. Please be still. I'm not going to hurt you.

A: I can't . . . I want . . . let me . . . let me go!

Q: Donatus—is that your name?

A: They—they call—call me—Doydoy.

Q: I don't want to call you that. Tell me how this happened to you, Donatus.

A: I—I d-on't know! I don't! Leave me al-lone—please!

Q: For God's sake, boy! I'm trying—

A: I can't! I tell you! I want-want my mother, fa-father! Mother, help!

Q: I'm afraid I just can't do anything more with him, sir.

Q: I care.

A: Aah, don't gimme that malarkey. Remember I know what's goin' on in your mind. Just the look of me makes you want to puke.

Q: I never—

A: You don't have to *say*. You haven't got it straight yet. Your mind's a piece of cellophane to me. You don't have to *say*. But it's my body and I'm stuck with it. I can do anything I like but change my body, 'cause I can't be sure it'd keep workin' if I did. Roxy Howard tried it an' killed herself an' I'm not gonna be that kind of nut. But if you didn't have me pegged down like this I could do anything I liked with you. I could change those brains you're so uppity about into cheese or jelly or lead. Then you wouldn't think I was so ugly because you wouldn't be thinkin'.

Q: You don't have to be ugly inside, LaVonne.

A: Anybody gonna worry what's inside me? Twisted guts. Them others, they make me laugh. So their old lady spits on them or their old man kicks them around. I got cheated before I was even born! Queen of Sheba coulda been my mother, wouldna made no difference. Ain't nobody in the world don't owe me something for letting me be born. An' I'm gonna collect. Every time, no matter what you think you can do with me. So don't gimme any bull that you care.

Q: I guess I've gotten all I want from you, LaVonne. But I'll tell you . . . you haven't gone deep enough into those layers of cellophane. I do care . . . and that's just the damn fool thing about it.

Shandy tidied the heap of closed files and closed her eyes against the face of X. It was an ugly face, a lonely face, radiating with the force of the psi to make its mark on Sorrel Park. Including herself, because she was here. She had told Jason she thought she could escape if she wanted to, but that was half-bravado, and even if she were free the problem would never die in her in the same way as she could get rid of Fitch and the bootlegging business. She was committed.

The ceiling light flickered and she glanced at it. The naked bulb in its mesh housing reminded her of Colin Prothero in his cage, and she shivered, and then yawned. Her time-sense told her it was one-thirty a.m., give or take five minutes; she was going to be terribly cross in the morning. She stretched her arms and yawned again.

And the light exploded.

Without thinking, she flicked off the bed like a lizard and rolled under. She waited there motionless for a few seconds, and then became aware of a stinging scratch on one cheekbone. She rubbed at it, and a sliver of glass came away on her finger.

She thought she heard noises outside, but nothing happened, so she crawled out from under and felt her way over to the window. She slid up the blind: except for a few misty stars there was no light outside.

A voice said, "It's okay. Don't get scared."

"Jason! What happened?"

"The lights went out."

"Is that right? I'm glad you told me. What are we going to do now?"

"Hold hands."

"Why Jason, I thought you were going to wait till I grew up."

"Come on, take my hand and I'll get you over to Grace's room. She's nervous and I want you to be with her while we scout around and see what's up."

She found his hand. The palm was not only sweated, but vibrating with such rigors it seemed the whole force of his body was behind them. "Jason."

"Yeh." There was a ragged edge to his voice that made her pause, but not for long.

"I know you wouldn't be scared . . . why are you shaking?"

"I just caught a chill," said Jason. "Come *on*."

Grace Halsey was huddled in her bed, and Shandy knelt beside her. "There's plenty men posted here, so don't get worried," said Jason, and he was gone.

"I am, just the same . . . Grace, do you think they've gotten—" She saw in the dim light that Grace Halsey, too, was trembling. She caught her breath. "They *have* gotten out!"

"Please, dear, don't—"

"But nothing can stop—why has he left us here?"

Grace fought for control. "They—you see, they trusted me, they know me, and they hardly realize anything about you; no-one has to worry about us. Really, we're the two people least likely to be hurt."

"Oh—I'm sorry, Grace." She was ashamed. "I shouldn't have let go like such a nut."

"It's all right." But the trembling increased.

"Grace, you're crying . . . ." Shandy touched the quivering shoulder, terrified.

Grace found a handkerchief and managed to control herself. "Shandy, I—I was a neurosurgeon before . . . the paralysis—and after that I thought I'd never be able . . . they asked me to come here and take care of those children . . . I—I trusted them. I hoped—oh,"—she blew her nose—

"I'm so silly." Shandy buttoned her lip. After a moment the voice came out of the dark again.

"My dear," Grace said sadly, "there's only one thing to be said about it. It's a mug's game."

sunburst: 7

SHANDY RAISED HER HEAD on an aching neck. She had gone to sleep crouched beside the bed. Her eyes were gritty. Grace was still asleep, fingers twitching, breath rattling in her throat. The light in the room was the amorphous gray ooze of early dawn.

Shandy pulled herself up by holding on to the bed. Her body felt broken in every bone. She looked up at the window and saw that two panes were shattered. One had burst while she was sitting there with Grace in the dark and the other must have gone while she was asleep.

When she put her head out through the hole in the window and craned her neck at the risk of slitting her throat she could see that huge doors had opened up in the ground by the walls of Headquarters, and men were driving tractors up ramps leading from underground storage vaults. They were dragging cannons painted in camouflage colors. After she had counted three of these she watched two tanks coming out and shook her head at what seemed to her the futility of the preparations. Then came several wheeled platforms stacked with antennas that looked like additional components for the Marczinek Field. Did Prothero intend to set up a mobile Field like a butterfly net, and shoo the Dumplings into it? She turned her head a little, and saw the mess.

The Dumplings, who could make nothing with their hands, or out of their angry lives, were prime breakers. They had blasted Marczinek's flowerbed down to the ground. A few blackened stems lay in writhing shapes, and the earth was littered with cinders and ashes eddying gently in the early winds of morning.

Something crackled and tinkled above, and she pulled her head in quickly. Another window. The Dumplings knew what was going on, and weren't afraid to show it.

She went downstairs and along the hall, gingerly, though she was sure Prothero was very busy elsewhere. In Urquhart's office she found Jason and Urquhart eating breakfast from a tray on the desk.

"Have some coffee," said Jason.

"I thought the electric went."

"Generator's going."

"Jason, Marsh's flowers—"

"Yeah. You oughta see what they can do to a human being."

"No thanks." She sipped the coffee. It was vile, but hot, and the heat loosened her joints. "How did they get out?"

"I dunno. We had a theory how they *might* get out but I can't get close enough to them to find out if they did it that way."

"Where are they?"

"Shandy, don't. Don't ask me, don't make me think about it more than I have to."

She thought of the Dumplings homing on his mind, on the minds of everyone here, except herself. "Okay." She turned to Urquhart, who was leaning over the desk and gnawing a thumbnail. "What are they hanging round for? They've been out over four hours."

"They were in eight years . . . I think they're trying to decide what they can do to really impress us. Something bigger than blowing lights and breaking windows . . . are you afraid?"

"I know they can't read my mind, and I don't think they can do much to me from a distance. If that's not being scared, I'm not."

"I am," said Urquhart. "It's strange; I've listened to people with the most irrational and fantastically ugly terrors. I couldn't believe I'd ever have to share in anything like that."

"Did you ever expect them to break out?"

"I'd given up expecting them to be good little kids."

"But how much hope was there for them? On those scores you gave them under Kaplanski's Standard Index—"

"There was a space to be filled in with a dotted line. I filled it."

"But you gave Colin Prothero a sixty-eight point four percent prognosis! That's just the sort of thing that's been encouraging Prothero to push for opening up the Sore and tearing down the Dump—and it's wrong!"

Urquhart crossed his arms on the desk and looked at her. "Shandy—"

"Don't, Chris!" Jason said quickly.

"It's all right. Shandy, Prothero's wife killed herself three weeks after the first Dump was set up."

"Oh."

"Yes; that crosses the *t* on Prothero for you. I knew her only slightly . . . she was a gentle person, but not a weak one—and she couldn't bear it. If that sixty-eight point four percent kept Prothero from going mad, I'm not ashamed of it. It was a genuine test score for a boy of Colin's age and intelligence. It just didn't—couldn't—take into account the fact that at the age of ten he was psychokinetic, telepathic, a teleport, and a pyrophore as well . . ." His voice lowered to a whisper. "Nobody knew it would last eight years."

"They're supposed to calm down in the mid-thirties—"

"What a hope!"

"—and Curtis Quimper. He was a late starter, so his burn-out would come even later. He's twenty-six now, isn't he?

"At the rate he's been burning himself out he ought to be practically ready to retire. But the break's changed everything. Before, I might have had some hope for him if he'd been man enough to duck the fight with the Kingfish—and managed to stay alive." He resumed work on the thumbnail.

"Grace is going to wake up in a minute," said Jason.

"Okay, I'll go back." He came with her, and she was glad, because the silence and the fear were palpable now in the empty halls. She did not feel panic, but she knew there was nothing for her to do here. Her usefulness was to have ripened slowly, but the time was gone, and the future terrifying. But it was not a thing to talk about to Jason.

Grace Halsey was not yet stirring, but her breathing had quickened.

"Is it all right to ask you how they might have gotten away?"

"Not much secrecy about that any more. As near as I can get it straight, it goes like this: while the radiations are circulating in the barrier, if one of the antennas wavers enough to get out of phase with the next one, even the slightest bit—well, that would leave a weak place in the Field, and they could all push through at once. It shouldn't happen," he shrugged, "but the Field's still working perfectly, so maybe it did. But that bunch of lunks hasn't got ten years of grade school among 'em, and they'd have to (a) know a lot about electrodynamics to figure it; (b) and be awfully sensitive to fluctuations in the Field; and (c) keep on the alert every minute,"—he rubbed his reddened eyes—"so I can't see how they coulda done it."

"You've forgotten Doydoy."

"Nah . . . I wanted to forget him. But what makes you so sure? You didn't know him at all."

"Another lonely kid? I think I know him. He'd have been reading everything he could get his hands on, and he couldn't get out to play. Besides, he's more than just bright. I bet every time you went into the Dump he was probing you down to the oceanic sense, blocks or not."

Jason grunted.

"Unless it was LaVonne. She's smart enough, isn't she?"

"Yeah, but she was never much of a reader."

"She had access to his mind. When they broke out eight years ago she was the one who shut Fox up. You have to destroy a part of the brain to do that."

"Broca's area . . . she got that from Doydoy," he admitted. "And so did I."

She bit her lip. "Damn. I guess I should have shut up."

"Listen, there's no getting away from it . . . but I always liked to think there was some hope for Doydoy."

"Oh, Jason! If you'd been in his place—"

"I admit it. I've never felt different. I'd have done the same."

"Do you get anything from the Pack at all?"

"They're a couple miles away—I don't know where—and nearly out of range. They can shield for a short time, off and on. Even if they couldn't, their group mind is kind of a mess, and it's hard to pick out a decent train of thought. A logical one. They never have any decent ones."

"Doydoy?"

"He can shield two-three hours—and I know what you're gonna ask: I can do it too, for about five minutes. Ever try concentrating on a pinpoint for an hour straight? That's what I go through each minute."

"Do you ever get any kind of signal at all from me?"

He sighed. "When I close my eyes you disappear completely. All I need is a pair of earplugs."

"Hey—" But her retort was cut off. Grace Halsey began to toss on the bed. "Shandy. Shandy! Are you all right, dear?"

"Here I am, Grace." The sky had been paling gradually, and now the sun broke between two lead bars of cloud with a harsh yellow light.

"Gee, I used to read a lot of junk about rosy-fingered dawn," said Shandy. "This one looks like brass knuckles. I'll get some breakfast for you, Grace."

The sun was coming into her room, but there was a jagged line of shadow on the blind, from a broken pane. She was lying on the bed. She had thought of getting some sleep, but a massive foreboding had settled on her suddenly. Since the situation had come to a head so quickly, there was no more time for her, and no more use for her.

She sat up and stared at the worn pale spots on the knees of her jeans. This room was not the young girl's dream, but she had never been able to afford many young-girl dreams, and for spaciousness, privacy, and cleanliness it was more than she had ever expected to enjoy. She could give up these but she longed to keep on drawing courage and affection from Urquhart, Marczinek and Grace; and she wanted Jason's astringent personality around. But she had no claims on anyone.

This was a strange place to have found missing parts of her character, and the qualities of home. But she was still far away from ultimate discovery in the first case, and permanence in the second.

"Shandy."

Jason was at the door, and he had a glum look about him. She got up and followed him silently down the hall.

When they reached the stairs she said, "He's kicking me out, isn't he?" He didn't answer. "It's no use, Jason. There's nothing for me to do here now, and he can't just hang around waiting and hoping to find some terrific talent I've got . . . Jason, don't tell me you're going to miss me."

"Me?" He glanced back at her. "Miss all that yackety— ah, forget it. I got used to you, I guess."

She didn't want to ask what plans Prothero might have for her; she didn't think she was going to approve of them.

Prothero was sitting at his desk, staring at his folded hands. He looked up. "Jason, I want you to go and tell Marczinek I'll see him in fifteen minutes."

."Sir—"

"Jason, keep your mouth out of this. I've told you what I want."

Jason disappeared with an angry pop. Prothero went on staring at his hands. He sighed. "Miss Johnson, we brought you here to find out if you could be of some help to us in the future. But with everything that's happened I need all the help I can get right this minute. I just can't spare you the time any more." He looked up.

She breathed deeply, hoping her voice wouldn't quaver. "Where do you expect me to go?"

"I'll have you taken back to your people. I don't think you'll come to harm."

"But my stepmother's in jail, the still's bust, and the rest of them . . ." Her voice trailed off. The rest of the Slippecs were hardly aware of her existence; they had nothing to spare for her. "I have no place to stay."

He said coldly, "You might find a friend to stay with. I'm sure you have plenty of friends. Or"—his mouth was grim—my friend Chief Casker of the CivilPolice will be happy to put you up."

"I'll find a friend," she muttered.

"Good." He began to shuffle papers on the desk and his face was so weary she pitied him.

"Look," she said desperately, "I can run messages for you. I could be useful that way. The Dumplings don't know I'm around when nobody else sees me, and I know how to keep from being seen."

"I can believe that. But . . . you are insolent and furtive. I can't have that here. I don't trust you."

"I can't say anything to that," she whispered, and turned to go.

She was throwing things into the duffel, lingering to draw out the last few moments, when Urquhart came in. She looked at him without speaking.

"Shandy, don't,"— he was groping for a word— "don't go to pieces—oh, I don't mean that, because I know you won't. But if you're anything valuable or special—"

"I could be a special kind of jerk." She gave the duffel-cord a yank and knotted it down fiercely.

He said, "There's a woman in the Public Library—a Miss Wilma French—"

"I know. She chased me out at closing time once or twice."

"She's really quite decent." He flushed. "She'd take you in if you told her I sent you. I'll write you a note."

She looked away. With the blood in his face he had given her a gift—his vulnerability. He had crossed the *t* on himself. But she could only shake her head wordlessly and swing the duffel over her shoulder.

And the noise began. A roaring that came from outside, and the quality of it made her drop the duffel and run out the door without stopping to look out the window. Urquhart was already down the hall. Noise washed and crackled around her, the walla-walla of a crowd scene in an ancient movie, the snick-snap-spatter of old sound track on cracked film breaking off and on in split seconds. She might have been a teleport for all she was aware of getting down the stairs or shoving aside anyone who was in her way. She ran straight into it, as she had run at the civvies. The experience had not taught her caution.

There was a milling of soldiers in the yard. Prothero somewhere yelling, "Get out that cannon, dammit, get—"

She pushed her way towards a circular cleared space near the flowerbed. Jason was in the center of it and around him, flickering there and away, yelling like forty, were four or five Dumplings in their prisoners'-gray, never the same one in the space of two seconds, flick-flick, there and gone God knew where.

She fought to keep balance in the push, and the ashes of the flowerbed crunched under her feet. She had seen the old pictures in the files last night, and she tried to pick out faces from them: here, Curtis Quimper with an aged and haggard face; there, LaVonne, a squat Velasquez dwarf bulky and grotesque in the coverall; Colin Prothero, Scooter, who had styled himself the Kingfish, Jocko; wild, unkempt, hair overgrown, filthy, stubbled faces scored with black lines as though they had burned their beards off hair by hair. Jason was crouched in the center with his eyes squeezed tight seeing everything and his hands over his ears shutting out nothing.

As she watched, he straightened, flung out his arms, opened his eyes and yelled, "Stop it! Stop it! Prothero! Stop it and shut up! SHUT UP!"

The Dumplings stopped, seven or eight in a circle, and flung their glances around the crowd like dust, almost tangible matter that left its influence where it was touched, and beyond.

Gradually, the rest of the noise stopped. The men became still where they were standing; two or three fell like statues and lay on the ground in stiff attitudes, with their eyes open. Prothero stood a few feet away from the circle, frozen in a flourish of arm movement, eyes and mouth open to the limit and face a slowly draining scarlet.

Then the Dumplings turned to face Jason.

He said, panting, "For God's sake, give me a chance!"

The Dumplings flicked out one by one like the lights in a sleeping city, until only the Kingfish and LaVonne remained before him. Like the rest, the Kingfish had changed from the urgent half-terrified boy who had run out in the moonlight with the Pack. His face had thinned and wizened. Shandy thought of the smooth-skinned children of the photographs; Marczinek's heart had turned at the sight of them.

The Kingfish was watching Jason speculatively, and Shandy realized she was the only other person in the courtyard who was conscious and able to move. But she stayed as still as the rest.

Jason lowered his arms and took a shuddering breath. "I told you I don't know."

The Kingfish snarled, "You're shielding!"

"I can't shield that good and you know it!"

Silence. If furies of argument raged and crackled inwardly among the three of them, there was no sign.

Shandy glanced at LaVonne. Her hair hung in long greasy strings and her hugely bulging forehead and cheekbones left only slits for the small glitter of her eyes. Her lips curled superbly up to her pug nose and her jaw was deeply underhung. Her uniform was as evenly tattered as if she had ripped it purposely herself, and she probably had. A picture of self-hatred.

Just the look of me makes you want to puke. LaVonne was another oddment of the Pack: a reversed spiritual image of Doydoy. Shandy recalled an old cartoon in which an ugly crooked man found a funhouse mirror that neutralized his ugliness with its own distortions and returned him a straight and handsome image. Left to herself LaVonne might once have found such a mirror—but not here, submerged in the raw honesty of telepathy and psychopathic contempt for deformity. Shandy wondered if the Dumplings ever got sick of their own transparencies and mutually perfectly-checked powers.

Finally the Kingfish scratched his cheek and said, in a voice that was meant to be persuasive, but came out a whine, "Doydoy always said you were a good guy . . ."

Jason put his hands in his pockets, waited, and said nothing. But his face was glittering with sweat under the morning sun and the dark stain was running down in lines from the armpits of his khaki t-shirt.

LaVonne snapped, "Come on, come on! We need Doydoy!"

"Ah, shut up, LaVonne! Listen, Hemmer—"

Jason interposed lazily, "Scared you won't be able to break enough windows without him?"

Whatever the Kingfish did was not apparent, but it made

Jason pull his hands from his pockets and hold his head screaming silently in a rictus of pain. Shandy trembled and was paralyzed.

The Kingfish said, "It's past the time for jokes."

Jason opened his eyes and grunted agreement. "I never figured you were joking. But I don't know where he is."

"He's gotta be somewhere."

"He's shielding." Jason felt the back of his neck, to make sure it was still there. "Maybe he's tired of you."

"He can't shield five solid hours."

"He might; you couldn't be sure." He licked his lips. He had made a mistake, and the Kingfish seized on it.

"If he can do that, so can you! Let's go!"

"Look, I'm not like that—you know me inside out! I—" But both of them leaped on him and had him down on the ground, face in the cinders.

"We'll turn you inside out!" The Kingfish, kneeling on Jason's back, spat and wiped his mouth on a shoulder. "Okay, LaVonne! Let's go!"

Shandy found voice, arms, legs, and finally sense. She grabbed a fallen rifle, knocked men over like dominoes, and leaped out swinging and screeching at the top of her lungs.

The Kingfish jerked his head up. "Hey!" The rifle swung. She had a blink of their gaping faces. The Kingfish raised his arm in an instinctive gesture that went back much farther than psi, sunlight flicked blue on the oiled barrel, and the rifle, coming down badly aimed, lost momentum in suddenly empty space and thwacked Jason across the backs of his thighs. The Dumplings were gone.

"Jason, are you all right? Did I hurt you? Jason!" She knelt beside him. He was lying with his face still half in cinders and his shoulders quivering. "Jason! What are you laughing for, you kook!"

Jason rolled over and sat up, still laughing weakly, gasping for breath, hugging himself and shivering. "I wish you could have seen your face!"

"If you could see your own you wouldn't talk!"

"That's not what I meant." Jason picked himself up and began to brush off the ashes. "I read a story once about some pioneer women larruping wild Injuns with broomsticks!" He doubled up and started in all over again.

She looked round. The yard was coming alive; men were getting up and moving about; they discovered that their eyeballs were dry, red, and painful from standing for minutes with their eyes open. Like figures in a sleeping-beauty pageant they tried to continue the actions they had left off, and discovered the cause was gone. The cannon gaped at emptiness.

Prothero's yell died down into a cough, and he began to make his way over to the flowerbed, blinking and rubbing his eyes.

Jason had stopped laughing. "Keep your trap shut," he told Shandy.

Prothero was shaking his head like a wet dog. He was still not quite aware of what had happened, and particularly that it had happened to him, Stephen Decatur Prothero. His hand came down with a hundred-pound slap on Jason's shoulder. "What did they want?" he barked. "Where did they go?"

"Doydoy got away from them, and they think we're hiding him. They didn't believe me, they were going to take me back with them . . . but Shandy stopped them."

Prothero gulped, and blinked painfully. "How did she manage all of that?" His hand on the shoulder tightened and corded, but Jason's face was expressionless.

"They put all of you to sleep—except her. It doesn't work on her. She was the only one who *could* do anything. With all the excitement, and being mad over Doydoy they didn't even notice she was there." He gave a brief and uncolored description of the wild lunge with the rifle, and added, "They don't realize she's just an Imper. Right now they think she's got some kind of psi they haven't come across."

Prothero swallowed in his dry throat again and turned to Shandy. His expression was as unreadable as Jason's. "Get back to your room."

As she went she heard Prothero asking Jason, "Where are they now?"

"Camping out by Pringle's Post."

"Hmph . . . right between us and Sorrel Park."

She sat on the edge of the bed and stared at the tightly knotted duffel. In thickly stenciled white letters it said, JOSEPH SLIPPEC USN. The very name Slippec looked strange to her, as though in the last three days her ten years of life with them had been blotted out. She felt numb. She had been granted a stay of execution, but what she was coming back to was not what she had only just learned to value. Her small security had vanished with the Dumplings.

Doydoy was gone. After eight years of hideous suffering he had still managed an act of defiance. Was he still the decent person Jason had once tried to help? And where could he hide?

She curled up on the bed. In an instinctive gesture she reached up and moved her fingers back and forth across the top of her skull. Her anterior fontanel had not closed until she was seven years old, and as a very small child falling asleep she would lie touching the faint depression where her pulses moved openly between brain and membrane. She had had the fancy that these were the thoughts moving about in her head. The Slippecs had not bothered much with doctors and no-one noticed the opening. It had not occurred to her how much more vulnerable than other children she had been, since a comparatively light blow on the head would have killed her—and blows fell like rain where she lived. Still, she had escaped.

Where was Doydoy? He had long passed the limit of his shielding ability. Suppose he had gone back into the Dump to hide. Unlikely. She didn't think Doydoy would want to see the inside of the Dump again even if his life depended on it —even if he had been able to get back in. Jason's esp range was two or three miles in radius, the Dumplings' perhaps ten . . . suppose he were a hundred miles away by now? Yet it seemed to her that a sensitive cripple who had been cruelly imprisoned for eight of his growing years would be terrified of the open world.

No, the Marczinek Field was the only barrier that would protect Doydoy. And the Dump was the only—no. She sat up suddenly. There was one other place, equally grim, and not really an escape at all. If Doydoy had used it, he would have been desperate to a degree that verged on foolishness. A place where he would be shielded—and perhaps starved as well. The Dump was impossible; this place merely crazy.

There was a knock on the door and Jason yelled, "Come on and have lunch!"

But she felt queasy. She had jammed herself down into a cleft stick.

I hope I'm wrong, because then it won't matter one way or the other, but in the meantime I don't know I'm wrong, and if I know my own brains at all, I'm probably right. In that case I've either got to tell somebody or shut up. If I tell, the Dumplings'll know about it right away and come down on us like a ton of bricks. If I shut up the Dumplings will probably figure it out for themselves in a couple of days— and even if they don't Doydoy will have to come out—if he can—or else, yell for help sooner or later, or starve. Now what am I to do?

Gee, sometimes I wish I wasn't so bright.

She opened the door and Jason said, "Just because you're a triple threat doesn't mean you need three times as long to wash your face."

"Some threat. They should know all about me anyway, just from reading you."

"They never believe me. I'm an outsider."

"They'd never want me as a sub for Doydoy."

"Not as long as they can't read you. He's their information-and-logic bank. Not willingly. They pump him when they want to know what to do and how to do it."

"Do you think he'd had plans to leave them?"

"I don't know . . . I think he might have been able to shield a plan to leave them—but I don't see how he could have hidden any plan to get out of the Dump—it was on their minds all the time. So when they were out he took his chances."

"I can't understand how they could have let me scare them off."

"You're an unknown factor to them. That's all."

An unknown, an x. She considered the two: X and x. The powerful but transparent Dumpling; the helpless but impenetrable Shandy.

"Wait, Jason." They were on the landing and she backed into the corner and leaned there. "I know Prothero's keeping me on because the Dumplings think I'm a threat. I'm no real use to him."

Jason raised a hand. "Don't count the teeth on a gift horse."

"Oh, I want to stay. I don't care how. Are the Dumplings reading you now?"

"Nah, they got their own troubles."

"Because you don't know anything. They must believe you that much. But if you did know—"

"Then *I'd* have troubles."

"He couldn't be shielding."

"No. Shielding's a kind of faint scrambler buzz you can't place or understand. You know the shielder's somewhere in range, you might have some kind of vague idea where he is, but you can't tell what he's thinking. With Doydoy now there's just nothing. I had to tell them the truth. Two-three hours is the most, and he got away from them that long before dawn."

"Then the Dumplings must know about your psi friends by now."

"Yes, but it doesn't matter. I told you they're not in Doydoy's class. Look, Shandy, I'm hungry and—"

"Wait a minute, Jason. Please! I have to know—is he still worthwhile?"

"Who?" Suspicion was growing on his face. "What are you talking about?"

"Doydoy . . . I wondered . . . oh—" She gave up. "Never mind. Let's go and eat."

He grabbed her arm. "Now *you* just wait a minute. I want to know what you're getting at. That look in your eye says you got something up your sleeve, and I'm damn well not gonna go through all that business like last night again. Out with it!"

"I don't want to cause any more trouble, Jason, I don't!" She was near tears. "It's just—I think I have a pretty fair idea where he is!"

sunburst: 8

THE PANDORA'S BOX was open. His hand tightened on her arm. "What do you mean, you think you know where he is?"

"Stop pulling me around like that! You don't like it when Prothero does it to you."

"This is different." But he dropped his hand. "Come on, if you got anything to say—"

"Do you want him back in the Dump? Do you?"

He grinned at her vehemence. "Pull in the claws . . . now look, you better get it straight. What I feel about Doydoy doesn't matter around here. Nobody gives a good goddam. What I think and what I do are two different things. If you want the truth, I think hanging around here and getting beaten up is one hell of a way to make a living. If you know where Doydoy is and we find him he goes wherever Prothero wants him put."

She lowered her head and started up the stairs again.

"Shandy . . . do you realize how much Prothero hates me?"

She stopped halfway up, without turning. "Colin's a Dumpling and you're not. What difference does that make? He can't hate every other kid in the world."

"It's not only that. I'm *like* him. I'm much more like him than Colin is. And I'm nothing. Nothing to him, anyway, because I didn't come from any long line of fighting men out of military and naval academies. My people were farmers and mechanics and my father left school at sixteen to operate a lathe in a factory. According to him I haven't any right to be his son's superior. *And he knows all this.* He's worked up a good case of high blood pressure, trying to suppress it. Jeez, I got nothing against him—I even like him. But it doesn't help."

"What's all this got to do with Doydoy?"

"Look, Shandy, I've got to stay here as long as I have the psi. If I try—"

"But he'll just get shoved back in the Dump, and the Pack'll find out and come down on us."

"I can't help that."

"If we could hide him—"

"How long could that last? Then we'd have to deal with the Dumplings *and* the MP—and there's no place to hide. I told you I can't leave here. And I don't want to have to run away from a court-martial. It's not only my family, it's my friends—and the psi itself. You don't know how it is to have this thing. I've got to learn how to live with it, and find out what it's good for, and I can only do that by being where the other psis are. I can't leave Sorrel Park and go out there where . . ."

Where it's so lonely.

"It"—he shrugged—"it sounds loony, but . . . it's my life's work."

"At least you know what it is," she said, not without envy.

"Yeah. It's one hell of a consolation. Now let's get that lunch. We can figure this out later."

"—could lob a nerve-gas bomb into Pringle's Post in two minutes," Prothero was saying.

"And they would be gone by the time it got there," said Marczinek dryly.

"They're too nervous to stay in one place anyway," Urquhart said.

It was true. The Pack was going to do something soon, and if it was too disorganized to plan without Doydoy it would lash out in irrational savagery—and not only within the small sector which had been shut off from the world for thirty years.

"It's hard to imagine Doydoy being able to hide from them." Urquhart sighed. "We could certainly use him working with us."

Prothero snorted. "You kidding?" Shandy stole a look at him. His eyes were still red and his face had a look of suffused fury at being hoodwinked by the Dumplings in the way Jason had never dared to do. "I tell you, if we ever get out of this mess it'll be a damn long time before I push for opening Sorrel Park again."

Marczinek said patiently, "The sugar, Jason, the sugar. I already have the cream."

"You never saw the inside of the Dump," said Jason.

"I never wanted to."

"Well, you're gonna see it now. It's the best place to talk."

"The guards will want to know why I'm going in."

"They won't see you."

She had the eerie feeling of being invisible, even non-existent, as the guards unwired the heavy doors with foot-thick windows salvaged from the reactor.

There was not a blade of grass in the Dump. The hard beaten earth had the charred look of the scorched flower-bed, and the gray weathered walls of the prefabs were streaked with flaky black. She had imagined a place littered with filth and rubbish, but it looked scoured by fury.

"They burn what they don't want," said Jason. "I guess fire's a good enough expression of hate . . . anyway, Doydoy isn't hiding here."

There was nothing there, aside from the buildings. Nothing.

"Even poverty puts out garbage," said Shandy. "What do they do for love?"

"Nothing I've ever been able to figure out. Even sex isn't love to them."

"Did they ever have any babies?"

"Babies! Urquhart'd've been crazy with joy if any two of them stayed together long enough to want a kid." He turned to the buildings. "Want to see the inside?"

She grimaced. "No. Why doesn't Prothero set up head-quarters in here?"

"Because if he ever cornered the Pack long enough to drive them in here, it'd be hard getting out on short notice."

"Jason,"—she scuffed at the hard earth—"this idea of mine might be all wrong."

"Maybe . . . but if you're right—"

"The Dumplings will know it."

"Yeah . . . and he'll let Doydoy rot here as long as Colin's dangerous. His life's work!" The gray earth. The blackened walls. They seemed to stain the sky above them.

"Suppose it was LaVonne or Quimper instead of Doydoy? Would you feel the same?"

"I'm half a Dumpling myself. I don't like the idea of any-body being kept in here."

"But Doydoy's so different—"

"Nobody will hurt Doydoy. You don't have to worry about that. But if you're right, and you tell me anything the first person the Pack's gonna be after is *me*!"

"I don't want you to be—"

"I know. I'm not whining." He rubbed the back of his neck. "But you sure are a funny kid. First you save me from the Pack, and now . . ."

She shrank inside a little. "You don't owe me a thing. Just get me back into Sorrel Park. I'll disappear and you won't have to see me again. Then you can forget what I said."

"No, I can't. It's a living problem, not just a lot of gobbledygook you can rub off a blackboard, and it's got to be lived out to the end."

"Then maybe I'll let you figure out for yourself where Doydoy is!" She was angry enough to add, "Maybe I haven't picked sides yet."

He only grinned. "Not even when you took a swing at LaVonne and the Kingfish?"

She said acidly, "If you'd been sitting on one of them, maybe I'd have swung at you!"

"I bet that would have been worth seeing, too. But I'm not gonna sit on you to get you to tell me where you think Doydoy is. I'm not that much of a Dumpling, and I haven't got time to waste. It's your decision. But if we find Doydoy, he gets handed to Prothero . . . now what'll it be, kiddo?"

"I—" She swallowed. She couldn't let Doydoy starve. "I should have gone myself. I could've—"

"Not without being seen. You're not inconspicuous here."

"All right. Come on."

Underground in the vault beneath the redbrick ell there was nothing but a vast expanse of flooring that echoed cavernously to the footstep. The ceiling was a tangle of pipes and wires from which the occasional electric bulb dangled, pocking the gray floor with scrofulous light. There was nothing left in the place but dusty tread marks where the tanks and trailers had ridden out.

"Over there," Jason whispered. He pointed to the dark corner nearest the ramp, and as she strained her eyes at it she began to see. It was there, knobs, rods, antennas and wiring. The cage.

"I guess I couldn't have found it by myself . . . oh well. It's on, isn't it?" She could hear the faint hiss and crackle of the Field.

"All the time. They run the connections underground to the Dump."

They moved silently toward the corner. Shandy's heart was racing, and it seemed as if its vibrations were replicating in the great echo-space around her.

Halfway there, they paused. A shape had become discernible on the cage floor. A blot of darkness, with nothing to recognize in the crumpled form but the great black boss of the hump, rising and falling against the crosshatching of the mesh. Doydoy was asleep.

Jason raised a hand, and they moved back. "You were right."

"I wish I hadn't been . . . there just wasn't any other place." They stared at the cage in its shadowed corner.

". . . I wonder if he's so bright, after all," said Jason. "There isn't any way of getting out of that thing from the inside."

"He was just awfully tired and desperate, I think."

"Yeah." He rammed his hands in his pockets and muttered, "I'll get Prothero."

But instead he moved silently toward the cage again, and she followed. He knelt beside it and twisted his hands in the interstices from the outside as Colin had twisted his from within.

Doydoy was sleeping with his body bent at an angle to conform to the shape of the cage. His limp legs were sprawled out like a rag doll's and Shandy saw in the dim light that the soles of his shoes were unworn. His face was pale and there were metal-rimmed glasses perched crookedly on his nose; a white blotch on his neck resolved into the bandage covering the sore Grace had dressed for him. His cheek was resting on his arm, and the breath sounded very faint and small on his lips.

In the opposite corner of the cage there was a food supply spread on a sheet of wrapping paper: a salami, three tomatoes, and a wax carton half-full of milk.

Jason whispered against the meshes, "Christ, I can't! I can't do it!"

She crouched beside him. "I'm sorry, Jason."

"Sorry! What else could you do? The Pack would have found him—or he'd have rotted before anybody thought to look here."

"What shall we do?"

"All my big talk . . . but I can't let him be shoved back in the Dump—and I can't let *them* get him. God, I wish I had power that meant something! Dumper's peeper!" He spat.

Doydoy had begun to stir; his arms were reaching out, and the muscles of his face were moving in small tics. "He's going to wake up in a minute." Shandy glanced about fearfully, as though the shadows were full of Dumplings about to spring. "Do they know anything yet?"

"No, but they'll catch on." He stood up.

She whispered, "Jason, if he sees you first thing he might get panicky and blow up. Maybe I could talk to him for a few minutes. Can you shield?"

He looked at her gratefully. She was giving him time, and the consequences of his decision could reach far beyond Sorrel Park. "I told you my limit's five minutes—maybe I could manage seven or eight." He backed away into the shadows.

She watched Doydoy, waiting as he twisted about as far on his back as the hump would allow. His hands moved, jerkily at first, as he pushed his fingers under his glasses and rubbed his closed eyes. Then they opened, a very pale blue that caught the light startlingly.

"Donatus . . ."

He came awake instantly, and his body rose in the air and flung against the cage wall like a wild thing. "Who-who are y-ou?"

His voice was cracked, and he was trembling so hard the wires rattled against the cage.

"My name's Shandy Johnson. I'm an Imper."

An understanding flicker struggled through his glare of suspicion. His body was half-fallen against the wall, hands flat on the mesh; his palms were thick and studded with calluses. "I caught a bit-bit ab-out you wh-en I g-g-got ou-out. Wh-at are you?"

In the scheme of things, he meant. "I don't know yet," she admitted, "but I want to help you."

"Why?"

"Because you need it. You can't get out of here without help."

"But why?"

She sighed. It was a wonder he could speak with any logic at all after eight years with the Dumplings. But he was no baby, and she couldn't waste precious time soothing him. "Because Jason Hemmer and I don't want to see you spending another eight years with that crew."

"Ja-Jason?"

"I'm his friend. He's always wanted to help you, and he's willing to risk everything to keep you out of the Dump. Will you trust us?"

He gaped at her like an idiot, and she could have sworn with vexation. But it was no idiot who had led forty-six people past the Marczinek Field, and there was no-one else who could have done it. She hissed, "For God's sake! Jason's over there shielding so the Dumplings won't know all this, he's given me seven minutes and I've used up three already! Will you believe me?"

Blinking owlishly, he raised a slow hand to straighten his glasses. "Th-there's nowh-where else to hide."

He had some sense, after all. "This place isn't safe either, now we've found it, and if we hadn't found it you'd have starved. Jason will find a way to keep you safe. But I can't let you out till I know you want to come, because *they'll* be here, and then everything'll be ruined. Will you? *Please!*"

He closed his eyes, and, astonished, she watched slow tears creep from under his lids to mark white runnels on his smudged skin.

"Doydoy! Donatus!"

He opened his eyes. Their pale color was the only clean thing about him. "Y-ou can c-call m-me Doydoy."

"No! I won't! You don't have to sutter and"—she slammed the cage with the flat of her hand—"you don't have to be in here!"

"I—I'm—I'm d-angerous."

Dirty, ragged, beaten down with suffering—dangerous was the last thing he looked. But the psi had given him more power than any one man had ever owned. "I trust you."

"Y-ou're an Imper."

She wanted to scream. Instead she took a deep breath and said earnestly, "Oh Donatus, you can't read my mind or pk me down to the bottom of a cistern, but you can throw bricks or cabbages at me and you'll find I'm as destructible as any non-psi in the world. I do trust you and you've got to trust me."

Before he could answer there was a hoarse cry behind her. "Shandy! Look out!"

She whirled.

The place was full of Dumplings.

They were not flickering; they had found a purpose and coalesced. She had not heard their sounds as they came, but now she was aware that the place had filled with strange echoes rebounding from the great bare walls. Some of them were in shadow, but some were in the beam of light from the doorway and they were looking at her. She glanced at Jason. He was standing still. He had put his hands in his pockets and his face looked as if he were doing his best to make his mind a blank; there was nothing else he could do. He waited there.

The youngest of the lot was fifteen. Curtis Quimper, the eldest, was twenty-six. The girls, shapeless in their gray coveralls, were as sullen and haggard as the boys. Jukeboxes, ice-cream sodas; not for them. It was impossible to imagine them laughing.

Curtis Quimper took a step toward Jason. "You didn't know where he was."

"I didn't then."

"Zatso?"

"Yeh, zatso."

She might have found this exchange laughable in another context, but not here. Their glances were flickering warily at her, and it was clear they were according her an enormous potential she didn't have. She was afraid to look at Doydoy. There was nothing to stop him from telling them she had no psi. If they had believed Jason they wouldn't have had to worry.

For eight years she had watched for signs of psi in herself without finding any, and without being very disappointed. Now she was beginning to understand Jason's wish for more powers, in the face of this forty-six-fold power of amorality.

There was a creaking in the cage beside her. Doydoy was pulling himself over to face them. The Kingfish strolled toward the cage; his look was sharp and cruel.

"Hey Doydoy, whatsa matter with ya? Aintcha been happy with us, kid?" The Dumplings laughed. Sound broke and redoubled harshly against the walls.

Shandy looked at the boy in the cage, and the sensitivity of her insights into Jason's feelings deepened once again. Hate and longing were mixed on Doydoy's face: the Dumplings were his siblings in psi if not under the skin. In the eight years of their relationship there must have been even for him instants of emotional unity so deep and strong that wrenching away meant leaving something of himself behind. Only the Dumplings had needed and respected Doydoy.

Yet he had broken away.

She breathed deeply and spoke to them for the first time. "You see how happy he was."

Quimper murmured, "You know a lot about it."

"I can see he's in a cage. I can see he was so hot to get away he didn't care that he couldn't get out." She smiled out of pure reckless delight, because the situation was so nearly hopeless. "It's kind of a funny choice for somebody who was so happy."

Quimper watched her speculatively. The Kingfish snarled, "What we waitin' for?"

Quimper held up a hand. "This is interesting." He said to Shandy, "You're not lookin' worried. Maybe you know something we don't."

"Sure, I know something you don't—and maybe I should be worried." She smiled again. "I'm just Impervious. You can't read me, but I haven't got any kind of psi at all. Not any."

There was a stir among them, and she disregarded both that and Jason's exasperated grunt. This kind of ace was not a card she could hold very long or play more than once. Whatever ability she had to help Doydoy now could not depend on imaginary powers.

Quimper had not moved. "What are you telling me this for?"

Shandy was almost beginning to like Curtis Quimper. She took another deep breath. "If I pretended to be something big you might be scared at first, but then you'd find out I was a nothing and you'd have a big laugh. I wouldn't like that. So I'm telling you the truth, that I am a nothing, and you respect me because I'm not cringing or whimpering. Except for power, it's the only thing you do respect. Maybe not much, but you're not laughing."

"That right?" the Kingfish yelled. He laughed, stupidly, in order to disprove her words; but it was an angry bark, and it echoed in uneasy stirrings among the others. They were tired of all this.

Curtis Quimper passed a hand over his face. There was a suspicion of weariness in the gesture, but nothing she would have depended on.

She said, "Maybe you better ask your friend here"—she indicated Doydoy—"if he wants to come. I can't talk for him."

A boy yelled from the Pack, "He needs somebody to talk for him, that's for sure!" and flicked his lower lip with a forefinger in an ugly wub-wub sound.

Curtis Quimper frowned and there was silence, but the Kingfish was certainly swearing with his eyebrows. "I don't like that kind of thinking, Scooter," Quimper said.

The Dumplings shifted their feet, and LaVonne laughed. "You gettin' old, Quimp?"

"No fights here!" Quimper snapped. "I ain't askin' for bombs." He gave his attention to the cage again. "Come on, Doydoy. We'll take your friend Hemmer, too, and we don't have to worry about spies."

He reached for the latch, and Shandy took a dreadful chance.

"Stand back!" she cried, and Quimper, startled, retreated a step. She put her hand on the latch and said very quietly, "I think Donatus ought to make his own choice." In a continuous unhurried movement she swung down on the stiff handle and pulled the heavy door open. "It's all yours," she said.

It was all the power she had: to stall and give Doydoy a few minutes to pull himself together and make his own decision; to startle Curtis Quimper—something only an Imper could do—in order to give Doydoy the freedom to act for himself. After that, if he went with them it was his own choice. And all of the blame would rest with her.

There was the stillness of a second, and Doydoy moved stiffly in the cage, drew breath with a shudder, and soared.

In the air he was at once commanding and ridiculous: a pterodactyl, or a Portuguese man-of-war, with his humped back and his limp legs dangling. But he was far from helpless: as he hovered over their gaping upturned faces, three riderless tractors plunged down the ramp, roaring and directionless; the Dumplings yelled and scattered as the tractors swerved, huge tires screaming.

Doydoy hovered for one second over the melee; then, almost graceful, he rose again and dipped down to land on Jason's back. His arms went over Jason's shoulders, Jason's hands reached back to pull the hanging legs round his waist; and, as one, they disappeared.

The tractors skidded and stopped. But the Dumplings had vanished one by one, yelling, emptying the place with dust-swirls to mark their passage.

All but one.

Shandy clung to the cage and trembled; dust settled around a crumbled figure on the floor.

She ran over and knelt beside it as a swarm of men began to pour down the ramp. It was the Kingfish. One of the tractors had crushed him and he was dead.

He was not going to lead the Pack.

sunburst: 9

SHE HAD BEEN shoved into a small empty office on the ground floor, and had nothing more to do than wait there, heels hooked on chair rungs, hands gripping elbows. Prothero had addressed a single remark to her as they brought her past his doorway: "Judas Priest! What did I ever do to deserve you!"

She heard his fury still boiling out of the office and along the corridors, breaking against the walls and washing like ashes and lava against her locked and guarded door.

She was neither ashamed nor proud of what she had done, but she could understand Prothero's point of view—for all the good it would do her. Jason Hemmer was more valuable to him than any other single person in Sorrel Park, Colin included. Doydoy was nothing to him, and she had lost him Jason.

For herself, in unloosing Doydoy she had contributed to the death of the Kingfish, a living person. She knew what it was to be afraid of psi now, not because she had felt its effects, but because she had manipulated it like a sorcerer's apprentice. Its danger threatened not only the powerless, but the psyche of its user. Only a psychopath could use it without damaging his spirit: a psychopath had no conscience.

Jason and Doydoy gone . . . if she could be sure they were safe it would be consolation in a comfortless world. Probably they had gone to join Jason's friends; probably they would find a way to take care of themselves; she would never see them again, and never know if she had helped them.

The door opened. Tapley was there, sardonic and pink-cheeked. She remembered him—he had taken notes for Grace when Jason was brought in to Prothero's office after the Dump checkup. Her duffel was swinging over his shoulder. "Come along. Prothero's got plans for you."

She got up slowly. "He's not giving me up to the civvies!"

"You wanna argue with him?"

"N-no."

"Then come on!"

The jeep rolled out of the gate without farewells. It was no loss; she didn't feel like facing Urquhart or the others.

She did want a serious conversation with Tapley, but the jeep was bouncing so wildly her teeth were chattering nearly out of her skull. There were only three-and-a-half miles between the Dump and the town. The late evening sun was burning down along the hills; it was too good and warm to give up for one of Casker's cells.

"No so fast, please!" she begged, nearly biting her tongue in half.

Tapley glanced at her. The open misery in her face must have touched even his stony heart, because he eased up on the accelerator a trifle. She cast about wildly, estimating the force of the thud she would land with if she jumped out.

"It's no use," he said. "I've heard about all your tricks. If you want to look at the sunset you better get Casker to give you a cell on the west side." And he speeded up again.

"Gee, Tapley, can't you let me go? I never did you any harm."

"No, and you're not gonna, either." He kept his attention on the road. It was desolate, with scrubby woodlots on either side, and barbed wire beyond them.

"You're not a very sympathetic person," she ground out between clenched teeth. They were approaching Pringle's Post, a weatherbeaten shed that had once been a fruitstand when jobs were good at the power plant and traffic passed in the mornings and evenings. "I thought the Dumplings were camped out here."

"Scout says they've shifted."

"I'm hungry. Couldn't we stop somewhere and get something to eat?"

"Nope."

No-one had offered her supper, and anyway she had lost her appetite at the sight of the Kingfish. But she was young and healthy and a few foodless hours had brought it back. Four days ago she had eaten with Jason at Jake's. The food was awful even by her low standards, but she had a feeling it was vastly superior to what she would get in jail.

"I really am awfully hungry, Tapley."

"Civvies don't starve anybody. Be there in three minutes."

"Three minutes!"

He slowed down again. "Look, kid. I gotta bring back a receipt for you from Casker. Neither snow nor hail nor heat of day's gonna stop me from delivering you and getting that receipt. I still got three weeks to go in this hellhole. I want to have my brainwash and get back to my wife and kids. You understand?"

"Yes . . . but I've been here all my life, and I don't want to be here and in jail too."

He glared over the steering wheel.

"I thought the MP didn't give people up to the civvies."

"You're a special case."

Special. "The civvies knocked in my stepmother's still— and bust her jaw besides."

"They might not do that to you if you're good . . . though it'd shut you up some."

She was ready to cry. They had already passed the market gardens and gingerbread houses of the outskirts. One minute, perhaps less.

She noticed suddenly that it was very quiet for a Sorrel Park Friday evening, usually a warm-up for Saturday night. She imagined a cowed and downbeaten people holed up like rabbits in fear of Dumplings to whom walls were nothing. There were no street lamps winking on in the thickening dusk; the men had probably been afraid to come out and repair the lines. And there weren't any emergency generators to switch on here when the main power blew. A few flickering lights in windows suggested candles or hurricane lamps.

The jeep turned along Main Street toward the municipal offices. Tapley began to whistle a tune. His plump pink face drawn up in a whistler's pout looked as innocent as a baby's. She had a terrifying vision of him vanishing out the door whistling like that while Mrs. Baggs the police matron was dragging her off to the slop buckets by the slack of her jersey.

There was plenty of space in front of the offices and he parked there. This place had a generator: a dismal yellow lamp burned in the fanlight.

She turned to face him for the last time. "Gee, whiz, Tapley, you wouldn't want to see this happen to your kids."

He got out of the jeep and stood there. His face was shadowed, but not so shadowed that his eyes did not show dark and angry. She had known she said the wrong thing as soon as the words left her mouth, not for their effect on him, but for what they did to her own self-respect.

"No," he said, "I wouldn't want this to happen to my kids. And it couldn't happen to my kids, because they're decent. Not as bright as you're supposed to be, but they're decent." She shrank a little at his intensity. "My kids wouldn't have been lugging bootleg liquor, or hiding in Prothero's office to steal his papers. My kids wouldn't have lost us our peeper. Now come on!"

She got out and pulled the duffel after her. His argument had hurt, but she thought she had an answer for it. She paused and searched for the sensitive in his truculent face. "You're self-righteous, Tapley. Your kids weren't brought up in Sorrel Park."

"Doesn't matter. Good's good anywhere."

"That's right. But you know what the civvies are like, and how they enforce their laws. I've done bad and stupid things, but I'm not sorry I helped Jason save Doydoy—and I shouldn't have to be treated this way. You figure you'll be brainwashed soon, you won't ever hear of this place again, and you'll never have to figure out what's really right and wrong in Sorrel Park. But I'm stuck here, and I have to do that every minute."

His lips were drawn tight. She sighed and started up the stairs, dragging her bundle.

She pushed on the heavy door, and it swung open, creaking. The hall was stuffy with the accumulated heat of day, and silent. The cooling winds swept in and began to whirl a small litter of torn papers on the floor; the doors creaked and swung closed; the papers tumbled and became still. They stood there, looking about. Then there was one strange noise.

Out of the corner of her eye she saw Tapley stiffen; there was a faint snap as he undid his holster. He took her by the arm and led her to an office door. The pane of glass was broken, and ". . . SKER . . . OUNTY . . . EF" with cracks running through it was all that was left of Casker's golden name. It seemed there was going to be plenty of work for glaziers in Sorrel Park if the place ever settled down.

"Looks like the Dumplings've been here already," said Shandy.

The noise resumed, coming from Casker's office. It sounded as though someone were bound and gagged in there, and Shandy cheerfully pictured Casker tied up in knots. Tapley pulled out his gun with his free hand.

"But they aren't around now, or you'd never have got to lay a hand on that."

"Shut up." He stepped into the doorway, pulling her along behind him. At least he didn't intend to use her for a shield. There was still a dim light from the windows, enough to show that the room had been wrecked, desk pushed over, chairs in pieces, floor awash with crumpled papers. Tapley replaced his gun and groped for the light switch. The generator put forth one more feeble light and they discovered not Casker but Mrs. Baggs on the floor, trussed and gagged like the pig she ordinarily resembled, hair awry and face a furious red.

Shandy said happily, "Well, that's not Dumplings—"

"Oh, for God's sake!" Tapley snarled. "Undo her."

Shandy hesitated. She would have been perfectly satisfied to leave Mrs. Baggs as she was.

Tapley allowed his hand to rest on the gun butt. She dropped her duffel, knelt down beside the helpless woman and began to pick at the knot in the handkerchief gag.

"Hurry up!"

"I can't go any faster, I'm breaking my fingernails!" The knot loosened and the gag came off at last. Mrs. Baggs spat and expressed her feelings freely.

"Save that. Who did all this—Dumplings?"

"Nah, we had that this morning. This is a buncha hoodlums turned the place upside down, grabbed Casker an' two others—gossake, git this stuff offa me!"

"Where was everybody else?"

"Some kook come in with a story about a riot over on Ticonderoga, Casker was dumb enough to send everybody out but us four an'—come on, I'm gettin' rope burns!"

Shandy rubbed her fingers. "They're all square knots—"

"I don't give a damn what they are, git'm off!"

No use putting off the inevitable. She undid them.

Mrs. Baggs pulled herself up and flexed her biceps with a will that promised revenge. "No use goin' for the phone. Lines are down." She twisted a knot in her hair as though it were the neck of a miscreant, and pegged it down with a fierce hairpin. "Who's the brat?"

Tapley was surveying the wreckage of the office. Shandy had moved away a few steps and now stared at the cracks in the dirty floor. Waiting for the ax to fall. She was not going to be caught dead making an appeal this time.

"Hah? I said, who's—"

"Oh—uh . . . just a package I'm delivering somewhere for Prothero."

"Hah?" The pig-face opened in a grin, remarkably like LaVonne's. "Valuable?"

"She thinks she is."

Shandy was numb. Tapley put a hand on her shoulder. "Come on, I gotta radio from the jeep."

Mrs. Baggs called after them, "Hey, when you guys gonna help us out with a few soldier-boys?"

Tapley turned. "Thought your blueboys wouldn't be caught dead having us around."

"Them? Them rednecks, their mas runs the stills. Listen, I could tell you—" But the doors were closing behind them, and they were out in the evening.

Shandy followed meekly, afraid to say a word and spoil everything. Tapley stopped beside the jeep and reached for the microphone. He spoke a few curt words, hung up, and dug in his pocket for a cigarette pack. He lit up, inhaled, and blew a plume of smoke out on the dark blue air. Shandy waited.

He stood there a moment, leaning against the jeep and smoking. Then he said, "Well?"

She blinked at him.

"You got friends here to take you in?"

"Yes."

"This place is dangerous, and it's gonna be worse. I can't take you back, but I don't want you running around the streets."

"They live near here."

He dropped the butt and stamped on it; sparks flashed and died under his foot. "Now . . . all I need is a story for Old Ironpants."

Treading on eggs, not to spoil it, she said very gently, "You didn't want to leave me with the old bat because you're too decent. Why don't you just tell him the truth, Tapley?"

He gave her one glare, jumped in, and gunned the motor. The jeep swung out with furious sound in the deserted street. She watched the taillights disappearing and there was darkness and emptiness again.

She parked her duffel in the nearest trashcan and trotted along Main over toward Seventh. If the Pypers wouldn't take her in she had no idea what she was going to do. There was no-one about, but the air was filled with urgency. With the civvies losing control the place was going to be full of life in an hour. She wanted to be out of the way, especially out of the way of hoodlums; it was not much fun matching wits with the witless. Dumplings were not extra bright, but there were plenty of interesting things about psi that were not shared by mobs and civvies. She would have liked to meet Jason's friends, but she didn't know where they lived, and had no right to bother them with her troubles, anyway.

She stopped and leaned against a wall to rest. She was dreadfully tired; limp and creaking. She sighed. She had seen and heard a lot, and learned something. She had plowed through books and spoken with Urquhart and Marczinek and the rest; she had seen the Dumplings in action and manipulated them, if only for a few moments. Now she had data to work on, even if it was shallow and fragmentary. She wanted food and sleep to feed her brains, and time to think and let her unconscious work for her.

She had chosen sides irrevocably. Prothero might not see eye to eye with her on the subject—she might never even see him or the others again—but she was committed to him and his Dump. She would find out what made Dumplings tick, how to handle them, what Margaret Mead would have done, and more. And when she had done that she would be a step closer to knowing what she herself was.

In the meantime she was only an awfully tired and hungry girl. She went on.

Stores and houses crammed into each other here, even on a main street, crowding the sidewalk. Sorrel Park, like many an ancient walled city, was composed of slums. But there was no castle on the hill . . .

She passed a faintly-lit window. It was the only illumination on the street and she glanced in, and stopped. The sash was up, and past the tattered lace curtain puffing softly in the night wind she could see two little girls bouncing on a big rackety bed with brass spindles. They were wearing nightgowns and had flowing black hair; they were only about five or six years old.

They had made themselves a world of peace and innocence for a moment in the circle of light from an oil lamp on a crate by the bed; and they were playing pat-a-cake in the furious and ancient plip-plap-crossclap of all children of Time. She had played it with the Slippec kids in her own time, and to the same song.

> *I'm just a small-town sweetheart;*
> *I love my familee, lee, lee,*
> *And after dark*
> *In Sorrel Park*
> *I'm happy as can be, be, be . . .*

Their voices quavered with every bounce, but they were extraordinarily clear and sweet on the foreboding air:

> *My father rolls the rubbydubs,*
> *My mother minds the still;*
> *I dance the jig*
> *In Clancy's Pig*
> *And my brother cracks the till . . .*

> *Oh, I'm just—*

A harsh voice in a foreign language cried out from within and broke the thread of their gaiety. The song trailed off, one of the little girls jumped up and blew out the flame, and Shandy moved on. They would soon be tired of that song; it was only a sober description of everyday life. But the silver thread of sound wove in and out of her thoughts: *And after dark/ in Sorrel Park/ what will become of me, me, me?*

She passed the silent crossroads at Eighth Avenue, and traversed a block in stillness unbroken except for the yowling of three cats in unreproved chorus.

As she reached Ninth the air began to tremble with a distant noise. It had the ominous quality she had felt in the previous silence. Two blocks up Ninth she made out dancing points of light that might be torches. She felt, rather than saw, that there were masses of people crowded on the sidewalk and raising their voices in the dark animal cry of the mob.

This was something ugly, something she was not going to run blindly into this time. She crossed the street swiftly and pulled back into the shadow of a doorway, straining her eyes on the long diagonal. The night was dark, they were many yards away, and there was nothing discernible from the distance. She moved up the street, close to the small shelter of the uneven walls. She remembered her resolve to avoid mobs and rioting, and it occurred to her once that instead of moving ahead cautiously she ought to be moving away expeditiously, but there was nothing going on in the whole world that she did not want to know about, and Sorrel Park was the world.

The crowd was milling about in front of a small low building. She recognized it: it was the Tabernacle of the Latterday Evangel of Sorrel Park, and normally housed a small bitter sect which had formed twenty-five years ago from the opposite end of the spectrum that produced the hoodlums and the Dumplings; it had so far been unable to send an evangel from its center. Fitch, a loyal fence-straddler, had belonged to it. Now the membership seemed suddenly to have swelled.

It was obvious that aside from the smoke and the noise there was nothing crucial taking place on the sidewalk; all the action must be going on inside, and she would never get inside unnoticed. And it looked dangerous. She watched for a few moments, trying to make sense of the indistinguishable grumbling. Shivers of sound echoed on the walls: "—outa here! Yeah, give'm the boot! What'n hell we waitin' for?"

Someone did not like the status quo.

The atmosphere was more dangerous than interesting. As she was about to move on with her curiosity unquenched she noticed one thing that was strange apart from the rest: one man was standing quite still, with his arms crossed, a few yards away from the others. His face was in the dark, but the position of his body indicated that he was keeping watch—perhaps for civvies, more likely MPs.

His stance made her uneasy. With his senses on the alert he would be the first to catch any movement across the street. One of the torches brightened and shook itself; the flare lit one side of his face, a mad half-moon. She could have sworn he was staring at her.

She ran. Turning the first corner she skimmed, awkward as a flamingo, past another deserted cross-street in a town of dark chessboard squares, past Tenth and down Eleventh, stopping finally at the first corner, a block above Main.

Quiet here still. She stopped to rest, breath searing her lungs. But the stillness between breaths was reassuring. She turned back toward Tenth; just half a block from the Pypers now.

At Tenth she peered round the corner of a rickety wooden shed housing a shoe repair. There was a distant angry murmur from the crowd, but silence around her. Then too late, she heard the creaking on the low wooden boards of the roof and somebody fell on her.

What breath she had left was knocked out of her, a hand twisted her arm behind her back before she could move, and as she wrenched her neck to squint upward something metallic raked across her face and caught a sword of light as it swung under the moon. It was a hook.

It caught under her arm and pulled her up, bruised and stumbling. She cried out, but her captor was wordless. She glimpsed him, a wiry man dressed in shabby working-clothes, narrow bony face, pale eyes, straw-colored hair growing like crabgrass.

One-handed and mute: a memory stirred. *You broke my wrist bringin' me in, Foxy, remember?*

LaVonne had shut Fox up for good.

"Fox!" she whispered. "What do you want?" But he paid no attention and she wondered if he had lost his wits to the Dumplings as well as his voice. With his good hand on her twisted arm, pushing in the small of her back, he propelled her down the street at a run.

They passed Pyper's Drygoods. The store was as dark and deserted as the rest of the huddled place. But there was a litter on the sidewalk, and close up she saw dark stains on the cement and scattered feathers eddying in the faint night winds. A few steps later she realized what had happened and stopped short. Twisting in Fox's grip, she bent double, retching emptily. The Dumplings had been here this morning; she knew their style. Having nothing better to do, they had killed Douggy's pigeons.

A memory of the birds flapping and cooing about his neck hit her like a blow between the eyes. Tears sprang from squeezed lids; she sensed more powerfully than a telepath the painful aura of Douggy's rage and sorrow. Fox pushed her forward roughly, and she stumbled upright. She had had nothing to vomit in her empty stomach and her throat ached.

At Main, Fox paused and looked back and forth. Satisfied that there were neither MPs nor civvies to worry about yet, he crossed the street and began the backtrack toward the Tabernacle deviously by lanes and alleys. She let him push her; she was too weak to yell. Besides, if no-one had been paying attention to three yowling cats in the full voice of the summer season they would not likely be on the alert to rescue her. She had no faith in the morality of Sorrel Park and the few people who cared about her were as far and unreachable as the moon.

She saw the mob close: rough men and screeching women at the Tabernacle entrance, but Fox got her through them in a mad drive like a hot knife through butter.

The air inside was hot, smoky, and fetid. The inevitable folding chairs were invisible under the hard press of bodies, black masses of ominous beeswarms. Fox shoved her down the narrow aisle leaving her to find footing among the outstretched legs. An oratorical voice from the platform boomed indistinguishable words vibrating on the heavy air.

When they reached the platform, Fox stopped, and she looked up for the first time. Three hard chairs were ranged onstage in a neat row. They were occupied—by Casker and his two civvies, all bound and gagged. The man at the lectern, mouth open and pale pudgy hands spread wide, was Fitch.

Somehow, Shandy was not surprised. Fitch at that moment stopped for breath, mopped his beaded head, pushed up his armbands with a flourish, and went on.

"Do we need it here? Do we need a Dump should have been blasted off the face of our fine city before it ever got started? Do we need an MP sitting on us thirty years, no decent food or clothes, no jobs, no new Tri-V or cars, a place where decent people have to go underground to get a little harmless entertainment?"

The crowd yelled, a torch flamed and scattered sparks.

"Do we need this Gestapo we got for a police force? Can't you and I and all the rest of the good people here find a way to run a city better than this?" Fitch certainly had nothing to lose, since he had prematurely cut off most of his liquor supply before Sorrel Park was opened.

As the crowd cheered, Fox, never once loosening his grip, reached over and tapped the side of the lectern with his hook.

Fitch blinked impatiently, lowered his arms from their embracing gesture, and bent forward slightly. Fox drove Shandy so hard against the edge of the platform her ribs nearly cracked—the gesture intending to convey the devotion of a dog bringing home the evening paper, or a dead rat—and stared up at Fitch with a dog's eyes.

Fitch glanced at Shandy and turned pale. He gaped like a fish for one second, then bent lower and spat through clenched teeth, "You goddam fool, what the hell'd you have to bring her here for?"

Fox recoiled and let her go. Shandy struggled to revive and straighten her arm, now almost paralyzed. Fitch's tongue flicked his lips. Breathing hard, he turned to his audience once more.

But in the small hiatus, Shandy, still rubbing her arm, yelled, "Hey, Fitso, you can't butter your bread on more'n two sides!"

She forgot her aches and pains and hoisted her way up on the platform by hands and knees. She was panting and breathless, clothes and skin dirt-smeared. The money, still folded in her pocket, had begun to burn a hole in her spirit, and the flame leaped through her body to her livid eyes. She was going to get her money's worth of something.

Fitch was a quick thinker. He sneered, "Who let you out of the Dump?"

Fox was clawing his way up on the platform, and Fitch raised his hands. "My friends, this unfortunate—"

Shandy was on her feet dancing out of the way of Fox's sweeping claw, and a woman's yell cracked the heavy atmosphere.

"Hey, Fitch! Hey Fitch! Wha'd she mean by that, hey? Wha'd she mean by that, Fitch?"

The voice belonged to Ma Slippec.

She rose, pulling herself out of a black clump of bodies, and climbed over close-crammed knees amid protests to the aisle. Her jaw was splinted in a scaffolding of slender metal rods, and beneath it the cords of her gaunt eroded neck rose like bridge-spans.

"Hey Shandy, it's yer ma! Don't be scared, dearie!" She broke her way down the aisle, elbowing, treading toes, waving her shawl.

Fitch lost control and screamed. "F'God's sake, Loretta, close your busted trap!" The name was grotesque applied to her person, dark and weathered as a blasted tree. Shandy had never thought of her as owning a first name.

"You don't tell me!" she screamed. "You made money offa my corn eight years, you gitcher hands offa my kid!" Her sufferings: the loss of Frankie, the broken jaw, the battered still, the miseries of a civvy jail—had gathered in this sharp moment to form a driving hammerhead. She would subside in five minutes, but while she was going she was a force.

Shandy was treading on Fox's good hand, and his mouth worked with soundless curses. Fitch moved toward her, but she danced away. She had no hope, but she had enough spirit left to be hopping with delight at the danger, the drama, and the corn of the whole rowdy scene.

Ma Slippec meanwhile grabbed Fox by the collar and flung him sprawling into somebody's lap. She jumped up on the platform and planted herself between Fitch and Shandy. "Go on, kid!"

Fitch was a man possessed. He would have wrung her neck but for the image he was trying to present to the audience.

Shandy was not anxious to be defended by this wild apparition, but she yelled out, "Who put the civvies onto your still, Ma? Who got your jaw bust? Who sicced the Dumper's peeper on me?"

Voices called, "Hey Fitch, what's all—"

Fitch howled, streaming with rage and sweat, "She's a Dumpling herself! She—"

Shandy hooked the money out of her pocket and swiftly folded it into a dart.

"Who got scared and gimme a twenty to get out of the way?" She shot the dart over Ma Slippec's shoulder and it hit Fitch square between the eyes. The crowd noise fell for a moment. Twenty dollars, in Sorrel Park's deflated currency, was something.

But Fitch had other lieutenants than Fox. Two or three burly ones were climbing over the edge of the stage. Shandy looked about apprehensively. The doors were solidly blocked. Ma Slippec, faced with a choice of attacking Fitch or defending Shandy, whirled about and clutched her fiercely, scraping her already battered face with the splint.

"Doncha dare! Git offa there, ye dirty bums!" But they were coming ahead anyway.

Fitch raised his arms once more. "Quiet! Please! We'll get this cleared up!"

Two of the men were already pulling Shandy and her protector apart.

Pop!

The noise broke like a shot, but more intense and peculiar.

And everything was still.

A figure presented itself, breaking the thick smoky ray of light from the projection booth. It was a young Negro boy wearing a checked shirt and frayed jeans. He was perfectly comely and ordinary except that his dirty frazzle-laced sneakers were dancing a good two feet in the air above the platform. His narrow ironic face was composed, but his eyes were sparkling, and the set of his body right to the top of his peppercorn head was so vigorous and joyous, and so utterly full of delight, that he seemed to be covered with spangles.

He pointed a finger as authoritative as Prospero's wand at Casker and his men: their bonds fell away. He reached a hand into the air, picked out three guns one after the other, and tossed them to the three civvies.

No-one else moved; the unhypnotized civvies were dumbfounded. He said, in a soft treble voice, "Come on, Shandy, what're you waiting for?"

Shandy's imminent captor fell to the floor with the snarl frozen on his face, and she climbed down numbly. The boy had landed in the aisle and she took his hand. They walked out of the door past the knot of living statues and down the street without any hurry.

She finally got her voice to work; it was feeble and squeaky. "Gee, I'm glad you dropped in, but wow! did you ever cut it fine!"

He sighed blissfully. "Boy, that was something I been dreaming of doing all my whole life!"

sunburst: 10

THE FIRES SNUFFED themselves, the noises died away behind them into murmurs and confusion, the night was dark. They ran past silent closed hives of red brick, round corners into quiet streets where the deep leaves of early summer rustled overhead. There was nothing to see of the boy but the white squares in the checker pattern of his shirt. She stopped, finally, gasping. "I can't run any more." She was doubled with a stitch.

"Listen!" he hissed. "You hear that noise?"

There was a small distant clamor not at all like the grumbling of the crowd before. "Downtown's full of MPs. I can't pk you an' I ain't gonna be caught in the street."

She clutched her side. "You go ahead. Tell me where I have to go and I'll get there myself."

He hesitated. Immediately a branch bent down from the tree above and swiped him sharply in the face. She jumped back, startled.

He grinned sheepishly. "Jason says he'll skin me alive if I leave you. Now come on!"

He led her through a maze of crooked streets toward the eastern limit of the town. If she had not been half-crippled with exhaustion Shandy might have laughed. Fitch had told her to hole up in the east end.

They finished in a mean street where the roads needed repairs, like every other district in the penumbra. The boy stopped at a white clapboard house; a picket fence enclosed a scrubby lawn with a small twisted apple tree.

As she stumbled along the path with him, and up the steps, the front door swung open with a haunted-house creak. She hesitated at the threshold.

"Gee whiz, what're you waitin' for now?"

She pulled herself together and went in.

The house had blackout curtains and was not dark inside, but there was a broad figure in the hall blocking the light from the kitchen.

Jason's voice said, "Shandy?"

The boy clicked his tongue in disgust. "Who else?"

"You all right?"

"Just tired." She could hardly stand.

"This prizefighter here is Prester Vernon."

"It ought to be Prester John. I'm grateful to you, Prester."

"Don't go gettin' all gooky over it," the boy muttered.

"That's no way to take a thank-you." Jason aimed a cuff at his ear, but before the blow landed he had disappeared and popped up again behind Jason's back.

"I can turn you inside out, Jason Hemmer!"

Jason folded his arms. "Helmi."

A young woman came out into the hall, and the boy cowered in earnest behind Jason's back. "This is Helmi Aaslepp," said Jason.

Helmi was a very thin sharpfaced girl in an advanced stage of pregnancy. She had blue eyes and fair, almost white, hair twisted in a knot back of her head. There was a vivid nervous intelligence in her face that Shandy had never seen in anyone, psi or normal, before. She caught Jason's grin out of the corner of her eye as she and Helmi measured each other down to the last level teaspoon.

"Glad to meet you," said Helmi perfunctorily. "I'll get you some supper as soon as we take care of this character."

Jason turned swiftly, caught Prester by the waist, lifted him up and hung him by his belt on a wall-hook between an umbrella and a set of oilskins. Unable to use psi against their combined forces, Prester could only drum his heels on the wall and scowl. .

"Look, superboy, it's not marbles we're playing here, it's a game of flesh and blood."

"Please let him down," said Shandy.

Helmi looked at her in surprise. "Why?"

"I don't want to get off on the wrong foot . . . I'm grateful to him for helping me. He doesn't have to be grateful to me for thanking him."

Helmi opened her mouth to protest, but Jason set the boy down. Shandy rubbed the crinkled head. "I got you off the hook but you don't have to thank me." Prester tried to keep the scowl, but it creased into laughter in spite of his efforts; he ran into the kitchen without a word. She added shyly to Helmi, "I'm not trying to get in your way either."

Helmi permitted the flicker of a smile to pull at the corners of her mouth. "Jason's told me a lot about you," she said cryptically. "You can wash up in there."

"Wait," said Shandy. "Doydoy is here, isn't he?"

"Yes. He's all right, but he's asleep now."

"Dumplings try to get him?

"N-no," said Jason. "Not yet." She glanced at him; something had closed itself behind his eyes, as though she were dangerously close to reading his thoughts. She did not ask any more questions.

Peter Aaslepp put down his coffee cup and nodded. He was a giant of same coloring as his wife; he had no psi, and his demeanor was full of the patience, humor, and tolerance he must have needed to live with a telepathic wife.

Hungry as she was, Shandy hesitated again. She had paid a great deal in emotion and physical effort to help Doydoy. She wanted, not a reward, but nebulously some kind of guarantee that he was alive and safe.

"What is it?" Helmi's voice was a trifle sharp. She was not accustomed to asking.

"I—I'd like to see Doydoy, just for a moment. If you don't mind."

Helmi wavered, but Peter Aaslepp said in a giant's voice, subdued with difficulty, "Let her see him, woman. She will not wake him."

"Come along," said Helmi.

Doydoy's face was pink and clean in the rose-shaded lamplight. His misshapen body was covered with a patchwork quilt; his hair had been cut, and except for the marks of glasses on his nose he had the look of the newborn baby sleeping with its soul retreated far behind sunken lids into whatever country it inhabited before birth.

Shandy had a moment of pure terror. In the cruel prison life Doydoy had lived with the Dumplings he had been strong and respected—if only for strength. Now he looked weak and helpless, and she wondered if she had only delivered him to the harassment of a savage world.

"Satisfied?" Helmi pulled the quilt a little higher, even though it was a warm night. The gesture declared that she had assumed full responsibility for Doydoy. "You can see we've been treating him a lot better than the MP or the Dumplings did."

No use in being jealous. She had no way of helping Doydoy herself. "It's not you I'm worried about . . . it's the rest of the world."

She watched them round the table as she ate; they were

waiting with her because there was nothing else to do. They were silent, but their communication was endless and unstrained by the intense hostilities of the Dumplings. They had a bond, stronger than that of the Pack, because it was composed not of mutually balanced forces but of affection, loyalty, and intelligence. She was welcome, through bonds of obligation—and excluded. She was different.

Yet, even as a close group they were individuals: Prester Vernon was certainly an ectomorph; Peter, phlegmatic now, might some day run to fat; Doydoy was ungroupable; Helmi was certainly like no-one else. But when it came to herself . . .

"Jason!" She put down the crust of her sandwich. "What happened to Ma Slippec?"

"I made sure she got home," said Jason.

"Gee, thanks, I'm glad of that."

Helmi said, "I don't understand your loyalty to that kind of person."

"She loves me," said Shandy.

The woman laughed shortly. "Call that love?"

Shandy hefted another sandwich and tested the contour of her stomach. "Her capacities are limited, but she does the best she can."

There was a glint in Jason's eye. "Dull normal?"

She had a sudden rare glimpse, rebounding from his eyes, of her own surface. "That was smart-alecky and I shouldn't have said it. She does love me. She risked a lot coming up on that stage to try and save me after everything she'd been through with the civvies. Not many people in Sorrel Park would have done it." A clock on the wall began to chime. It was eleven, but the others looked as if they were going to stay up all night. "Do you live here, Prester?"

"Yeah, but not so's anybody'd notice."

"We keep out of the way," said Helmi.

"I can understand that," she said, "but why stay here?"

"Where's a better place to start?" Helmi asked.

She was silent. She did not really want to know if they intended to save the world, starting with Sorrel Park. Not now; she was too tired. But there were plenty of unanswered questions waiting.

She bedded down on the chesterfield with a blanket, too sleepy to eavesdrop on their still murmuring voices from the kitchen. Her last feeling before falling asleep was of that palpable sense of exclusion. She was alone. Again. She realized that what she was feeling was the *return* of that sense. It had been with her all her life until those few days at the MP depot, and there it had left her so painlessly she hadn't realized it. But the return was painful, because there was no place for her here either. She slept.

Momentarily the surface of her sleep was broken by a shout in the street but it did not disturb her as much as an ominous calm, an undercurrent of wonder that the Dumplings weren't trying to grab Doydoy, and that no-one here was worried about it.

On a level deeper still, in some vault of her unconscious, logic was beginning to collate data.

She slept on in the eye of the hurricane.

She woke in early dawn with a gritty residue of weariness, to the sound of voices still coming from the kitchen. She stretched cautiously, feeling almost hamstrung. Her ribs ached from being knocked about, and her face was raw with scratches.

Helmi's voice from the kitchen said clearly, "—can't go on like this."

Like what? Shandy sat up and swung her legs down. Her clothes were filthy, but she was stuck with them. She pulled her old sneakers on; the only respectable articles of clothing she owned were the laces Jason had given her the night before last.

"And there's the other problem," the voice went on. "What to do about *her*."

Shandy pricked her ears, thought better of her intentions, and yawned loudly. The voices shut up.

She dragged herself into the kitchen. They were in the same positions around the table, and she did not know whether or not they had slept. "Where's Doydoy?"

"Still asleep," said Peter.

She looked round at them all. She had come to a hard decision, and she silently awarded herself the razz for her sense of its altruism, without stopping the ache. "I'm going to leave, Jason. I'd like to thank you for everything."

Jason's mouth fell open. "When the hell'd you make that big decision?"

"Last night. It's no good my staying here. Maybe I'll be useful some day, but if I hung around here now you'd probably spend all your time keeping me out of trouble.

You got a lot to do and you need me like a hole in the head."

He slapped the side of his head. "I got a hole there already! My brains are falling out and I don't know what you're talking about. You can't go running around in that pigsty!"

"I know my way around. Jason," she said, "let's face it. I'm nothing here."

Jason glared round at the others, but Peter only said, "Let her go, Jason, if she is unwilling to be here. You can see that she reaches home safely."

"She has no home," said Jason. "You sit down."

"Yes," Helmi sneered. "She may be no use to us, but she could be a dangerous use to the Dumplings. I'd rather have her here where we can keep an eye on her."

"Stop that! You know that's not why I want her here!" Helmi shot him an ironical glance.

Shandy said awkwardly, "Thank you, Jason. I—I'm glad you like me, or think I'm valuable, or feel responsible for me . . . but it would be wrong for me to stay." She turned to Helmi. "I don't intend to help the Dumplings. Even if I did and you wanted to keep me here you'd be far too busy to make it worthwhile holding onto me."

Helmi stood up to pile dishes. "Would we have to?" Her eyes were icy. "Have you ever read *Odd John?* You might remember an incident in which John was caught in a theft by a policeman and killed him rather than be endangered by exposure . . . his argument was that in comparison with him the man was an animal, and every human has the right to kill an animal in self-defense."

Peter was staring at her in horror and Jason in exasperation, but Shandy had seen her hand moving around her swollen belly, and said, "I think every woman would feel she had the right to do something drastic to save her baby— but that's a filthy argument to base an ethic on. In John's own terms, first he baited an animal, and then killed it because its rage endangered him." She snorted. "No wonder his species ended blowing themselves up!"

Peter was still staring at his wife. "I hope you did not mean it, woman."

Helmi's lips trembled. "I didn't mean it." She covered her face with her hands.

Jason said gently, "Come off it, Helmi. You only got what you gave."

"I've done it again," said Shandy. "I didn't mean to hurt you, but you can see I can't stay."

"Sit down," said Jason. But she was heading for the door. He roared, "Siddown!" and slammed the table so hard the dishes rattled. She came back and sat down meekly.

He mopped his red face. "You just told me you were glad somebody cared? Well, we'll be needing you too before this is over. Now eat breakfast."

"Jason. I wouldn't—you don't think I'd help the Dumplings?"

"Oh, for God's sake! Maybe someday we'll have to kill some animals, but we'll damn well make sure we know what's an animal first."

Helmi wiped her eyes. 'You don't care what happens to us." Her voice shook. "Hiding all these years, and now I've got the baby coming, letting yourself get beaten up so nobody respects you and everybody so scared of psis they wouldn't believe one in a thousand years! Now you let Prester show himself and put us into more danger, and all for her! Why? Why should we care if one brat lives or dies?" She jumped up from her chair and ran into the bedroom, sobbing. Peter followed her in, shaking his head, and Prester picked himself up and went out to the back porch.

Shandy looked thoughtfully at the closed bedroom door. Jason was picking crumbs off the tablecloth. He raised his head. "You got that look in your eye again."

"I never said a word."

"Come on, out with it. I know you."

"First . . . why do you have faith in me, Jason? It can't be anything really important, or Helmi wouldn't have gotten so mad."

"Only an idea, been kicking around in the back of my mind. I'll let you know when there's something definite to tell you. Helmi knows what's important, all right. Now you tell me what you're stewing about."

"Oh . . . I know you're not loyal to Helmi and Prester only because they're psis; you love them too. I trust your judgment. If you find Helmi lovable and I can't, there must be a good reason why she's acting so unlovable right now."

He looked at her from under the eave of his brow. "You're sure there has to be?"

She replied modestly, "I've generally found it to be so in my experience." He snickered. "You'll notice," she said, "I'm not asking."

"Yeah, yeah, I notice. You got signs hung out all over you." He dug out his cigarettes in their crumpled pack, lit one, and blew smoke at the ceiling. Then he leaned back in the chair with his arms crossed, thinking. When he had settled something to his satisfaction, he grunted and said, "You remember Curtis Quimper was the first person to discover he had psi."

"Yes."

"Well, Helmi must've been a close second. I don't have to bother with the whole story—her parents died of radiation and her background's a lot like yours. She wasn't like you, though . . . she was a scared wisp of a kid, and finding out about the psi gave her a real jolt. She didn't know what to do with it or how to handle it and she was terrified. And before she had time to get used to it, Curtis Quimper found out about her . . . and he figured he'd have some fun. You can imagine."

"Yes . . ." She shivered.

"He made it rough for her, all right. She was too scared to fight back and she knew if she told anybody they'd think she was crazy. After a while she got so paralyzed with fear she wouldn't move out of her room, and nobody could figure out what was wrong or what to do with her. The people she lived with were thinking of having her certified. Luckily—for her—all the rest of the psis woke up nearly together, and grouped. Quimper forgot his games when he found himself running at the head of the Pack. They couldn't have dragged her along with an atomic sledge by then, she was so knotted up. When they got put away she managed to pull herself together, too scared and broken up to get out and start over outside, and terrified that if she stayed and were found out she'd get shut up in the Dump—with them. But she found Prester and me after a while . . . and I guess you understand a little better now."

"I'm sorry. I should have kept my mouth shut."

His brow curled and quivered. "I didn't think you were such a sensitive little thing! If you hadn't wanted to know I'd have been disappointed in you."

She remembered Prothero's scene with Colin. "That's awfully private. If my knowing about it hurt her—"

Jason shrugged. "All the Dumplings know it. That hurts. But my knowing, and Peter and Prester . . . you're with us, and you've read all the files. She doesn't mind, in spite of what she's said to you, or I wouldn't have told you."

He had said: you're with us. She coughed to conceal her mingled pleasure and embarrassment. "I can see why she just wants to lead an ordinary life, and why she's so upset now the Dumplings are out. And I can see why you all stayed around here, too, but I think you crippled yourselves unnecessarily."

"I guess we did—in the way a very strong person has to be careful about using his strength. But we have to forget about the past now; it's the future that counts."

She looked at him searchingly. "Were you really very anxious to go out and save the world?"

"I had some daydreams."

"No burning ambitions?"

"I always knew I didn't have enough psi to make me king of the castle, so . . ." He watched while she took a piece of cold toast and delved rather deeply into the butterine. His voice was casual. "I enjoy your little roundabout excursions, but with time running short maybe you better get down to what you really mean to say."

But she was thinking deeply and not to be hurried. "How many psis would you put in the genius class?"

He scratched his head. "It's so hard testing psis—or even Impers . . . I'd put Doydoy up there; LaVonne, maybe, if she knew how to handle her brains. Prester's an irresponsible kid, but I'd take the chance and put him between the two of them . . . Helmi and I come well under them, and after us there's nothing at all, because all the rest of the Dumplings run from about 75 to 110. Now what's next?"

"People have always thought of psi as something super-human . . ."

"Yeah. So what?"

"You said once that most normal people have vestiges of it, telepathy, at least, but it's stronger in babies and kids because they can't express themselves very well by talking. Pk and tp don't seem to occur naturally . . ."

"Keep going."

"So if there's any everyday kind of psi it's telepathy in babies and kids . . . maybe herd animals, too, and ants?"

"I'll buy it." He folded his arms and watched her with the wary look he reserved for her. "And?"

"When it finally came to people as a radiation mutation it hit juvenile delinquents."

He said in disgust, "Tell me something I don't know!"

"Jason . . . what have they got in common?"

He stared at her for a moment. Then he said "Ow!" and clapped his hand over his mouth.

"I didn't mean—" she began.

He said grimly, "Didn't you! Helmi, Pres!"

They appeared in their chairs at once, Helmi red-eyed but composed to the point of chill. Their double noise was excruciating. Shandy said in a small voice, "Please don't do that, it scares me." Peter shambled out of the bedroom, bewildered.

Helmi said, "You'd better put that clearly."

At this point, she didn't want to. But she took a deep breath, and said, "Psychopaths have brainwaves like children . . . a sentence in a book I read about juvenile delinquents stuck in my head: *Their minds seem more primitively organized.* That's what they've got in common with all the other creatures in the world that have psi." She looked at them, but their faces were expressionless. "I've been trying to say: psi might be nothing but an ability that belongs to animals . . . for civilized people, just interesting garbage. Maybe . . . maybe you were banking on being considered superior because you have psi, you're not psychopathic, and you're a lot brighter than most of the Dumplings? . . . this might hurt you a bit, but maybe you'd even be a little relieved? Not to be responsible for the fate of the world?" She turned pleadingly to Jason. "I don't think you'd mind terribly, Jason? You're an unpretentious person."

He stared at her, half-outraged for a moment, and burst out laughing till the chair rocked under him.

Helmi's face thawed a little. "You have a genius for the left-footed compliment."

Peter took her hand. "I will mind for you, if you like."

"It's all right, Peter. I can manage. But I'd like to know why I'm sitting here letting a thirteen-year-old kid tell me all my talents and powers are trash."

"You didn't care for them very much anyway, Helmi," Shandy said.

"Even if your wild logic holds together," said Jason, "which I doubt, what you're mainly doing is calling the Dumplings animals. It's kind of a way-out asumption."

Shandy said impatiently, "I'm trying to say that the psychopath started out being one in his mother's and father's chromosomes. People see a healthy-looking kid with average intelligence and a healthy mind and nothing missing but a conscience, so they figure he was brought up wrong. But I don't think he was. I think he had something wrong before he was born, like a mashed-up chromosome, or one too many, like the mongoloid . . . and maybe it made him slide a quarter-inch back down toward Neanderthal."

sunburst: 11

Prester Vernon yawned, "You shootin' that off the top of your head?"

"Well, I was kind of thinking on my feet," she admitted, "but all the bits of the idea were hanging around waiting to be put together."

"They may never stick together," said Jason. "That Neanderthal bit won't be popular with the parents of these kids."

"Many of them are a lot like the kids—and the rest think they've done every wrong thing in the book bringing them up. Wouldn't this be easier to take?"

Helmi said thoughtfully, "Everyone says amoral people are animals."

"Yes, but they don't mean it. Prothero said it to Colin: 'You're in a cage because you're an animal.' But he meant acting like an animal, not really one. Gee, I'm not trying to say they belong with the monkeys in the trees."

"Even if you could prove it for the Dumplings," Jason said, "you'd have a heck of a time trying to sort them out of the ordinary lot. There's so many borderline cases, how could you define the animal?"

"The psi did it for the Dumplings, but it would be hard, picking them off all over the world. The Prognostic Index might help, but you can't test very young kids."

"And they usually have the brainwaves of children, too."

"Yes, darn it, and you can't pick them out at birth."

"No, you'd have to wait till they started busting a few windows," said Jason.

"If they're mesomorphs—present company excepted," she added hastily.

"We'll worry about that later," said Jason. "Keep on defining."

"Well . . . you sift out mesomorphs who've gotten in trouble with the police a lot as young kids, and have low indexes. Most of them come from families without very strong morals—often immigrants who have trouble coping

117

with a new country. Maybe some of them have moved because they can't get along very well in their own countries. I've heard poverty is a cause of delinquency, but I think these kinds of shiftless, helpless people could be a cause of poverty too . . ."

"Most of the psis are boys," Helmi said, "and most delinquents . . ."

"Girls don't throw themselves around so much. They don't rebel by stealing cars—but they can find plenty of other ways to mess up their lives . . . and remember how scared you were when you discovered you had psi, Helmi? Maybe there's a few girls yet in Sorrel Park who have psi and never got frightened or angry enough to open it up inside them."

"That gang business is an animal thing, I think," said Jason.

"Oh, yes . . . I once read a zoologist's description of a couple of bunches of apes—what he called primate hordes—threatening each other on the borders of their territories, and it sounded very familiar. The parents're always saying, 'My Joey was such a good boy till he started running around with that gang.' They never figure that's what their Joey was waiting for all his life—some of his own to run with, and a herd leader instead of an old drunk of a father. And something to bust. They can't get along with ordinary people. The world's a zoo to them, and they have to throw themselves at the bars."

"Yeh . . . I guess there's no place in the world for them to be free. But how do you tie all this in with the psi?"

"I can't completely. But most of the Dumplings were born to people like the Slippecs, the kind who often have delinquent kids. And at least one of the two parents had had a lot of radiation and didn't have the Dumplings till he was over forty. The mongoloids and the kids like LaVonne and Doydoy usually get born to that group, because they're just getting too old to have healthy babies—and the radiation was one more strike against them. So they ended up with psi."

"Then you say that since psi is an animal function, this exaggerated psi the Dumplings have is a logical result of radiation-induced mutation—in what *you* call a human animal."

"Gee thanks, Helmi. That's just what I *have* been trying to say."

"You don't think much of psi," Jason said.

"Well—it's a mutation, and from what I've read, most mutations are harmful; a mutation's a good thing only if you can't get along without it in your environment—or at least it shouldn't do any harm. I think it's done a lot of harm, and I think the world can get on fine without it. You don't have to walk through walls too often in the ordinary run of life, and if you need to haul a ton of lead you can use a freight car. I guess scientists and surgeons could use the pk—but they haven't got it. Dumplings have it. Besides all that, it takes a lot of energy. Doydoy's stunt yesterday seems to have taken a lot out of him."

The others stirred in their chairs, uncomfortably. So there were still things she didn't know, and she was going to have to wait for them to volunteer the answers.

"Now," said Jason, "I think I'd like to know where *we* come in with all this. In your theory."

She wriggled a little under their scrutiny. In spite of their good intentions, they were a powerful group of people—with ordinary emotions, not those of supermen, and she was extremely vulnerable. She said carefully, "You can find plenty of use for psi. If you could use it to examine the Dumplings as they ought to be examined you might be able to prove—"

He jeered, "Come on, you know that's not what we're talking about. We want to know where we fit in with your dinky animal theory. Better start thinkin' on your feet again!"

She snapped, "You said a while ago you'd want to know what was an animal! Didn't you? I've been trying to define it. But I don't know how to account for you and I couldn't do it grouping you with the Dumplings."

"Not safely."

"But if you can work up a theory that takes care of forty-five psis out of fifty it shouldn't be thrown in the garbage. I can't call it a theory, it's only an idea—a way to look at things from a different direction. I don't know why Prester and Helmi are psis. Doydoy and LaVonne aren't animal types, but I guess Urquhart would call LaVonne a psychopath. And you're a mesomorph way past the Dumpling type, Jason. Maybe you're something special."

Jason looked up and asked the ceiling, "Hey Fitso, who's the monk on the lamppost?"

She said in a fury, "Maybe I remember something too!

Something you said yesterday that—that—" She trailed off.
Maybe it was time to begin learning not to shoot her mouth
off. "Oh, forget it."

"It's too late for that now," said Jason. "Go on, tell me
the horrible thing I said."

She swallowed. "You said, 'I'm half a Dumpling myself.'"

He grunted, and Prester Vernon snickered.

She added gently, "You also said, quote, 'It's a living
problem, not just a lot of gobbledygook you can rub off a
blackboard, and it's got to be lived out to the end.' I don't
care if you throw the idea out the window, but you do
have to consider it as a possibility in the problem of psi—
and it's part of living it out to the end."

"So okay, we'll leave it at that. But now we've talked
about us maybe you've got an idea where *you* come in?"

"I think that's Urquhart's department, Jason . . . maybe
yours too. You hinted about something a while back. But I
won't ask now . . ." She was suddenly leery of that problem.

"Not ask! Maybe you're not too keen on finding out!"

"Oh, I know how you feel. I *have* to find out, sooner or
later. I might not like it when I do. If you know something
that'll hurt me—maybe you feel like hurting me right now.
I know I'm clumsy and irritating sometimes, but—but I
love all of you and I haven't meant to hurt you."

They looked at each other and sighed. Prester Vernon
snickered again. "Shandy, you sure lucky nobody ever
thought to clunk you on the head and split your skull for
being so smart."

"Maybe I can learn a little tact now I've got to this age,"
Shandy said, laughing. She touched the top of her head. "I
am lucky no-one tried it because my fontanel didn't close
till I was seven and I bet the bone's still kind of feeble up
there."

They stared at her. Jason said, "Why didn't you mention
that to Grace or Urquhart?"

"I—I thought it was just a kind of freak thing that
happened to grow that way. Does it mean anything?"

Jason rubbed his head. "I wonder . . . there was a term—"

"Extended foetalization," Helmi said.

"Oh. Does that mean it's going to take me another thirteen
years to grow up and then I'll be six-foot-seven?"

"Nope," said Jason. "By your own statement you had
most of your growth up to twelve and then started slowing

down, so the prolonged infantile part—if that's what it is—
is probably over. Physically." He smothered a surge of
laughter and added gravely, "Anyway, Grace thinks you
should start becoming interested in boys any day now."

Shandy sniffed. "Did she say when she thought I was going to become interesting?"

"If we ever get out of this mess," Helmi said smiling, I'll
treat you to a lipstick and fix up your hair for you."

"Oh, no! Don't do that!" Jason cried. "She might turn out
beautiful, and then she'd be really unbearable! Ouch, help!
Hey, get her offa me!"

"Jason! Shandy! Stop it!" Helmi jumped up and pulled at
Shandy, who was attacking Jason with a dishtowel. "Stop it!
Something's wrong!"

Shandy stepped back. "What—"

Silence, except that the clock ticked with flat measured
strokes.

In the street a child was bawling: "But I dowanna stay
inside!"

"My God!" Jason pulled himself up slowly. "I'm a dope.
Horsing around and . . ."

Shandy and Peter gaped at him. "What is it?"

"The Dumplings. No buzz . . . they were camped in the
woodlot, shielding. Now they're not. There's no scramble,
nothing coming from them at all. They're gone!"

"Out of Sorrel Park?"

Jason muttered, "Gotta get back to Prothero—oh boy, is
he gonna boil me in oil. No use, Helmi, you can't come."

"No, she cannot," said Peter.

"I—I—" Helmi twisted her hands, glancing at the boy.
"Jason, he's so young." Prester made a face at her.

"Maybe we won't need him," Jason said. "I'll go first, anyway. Mind *you* keep out of it, now!" He gave Shandy a
sharp fierce look as if to pin her to the spot. She blinked,
and he was gone by the time her eyes opened.

Helmi sank down at the table. Prester was staring out of
the window. "Doydoy—" Shandy began.

Helmi said, "There's no use keeping that a secret any more
. . . Doydoy's gone too, for all practical purposes."

Shandy whispered, "Not dead?"

"No, not dead. But he might as well be. He's not sending
and he's not receiving, and he won't move or speak. He's as
impenetrable as—as you are."

"But why?"

"He says he killed the Kingfish and he's going to fry in hell for it."

"But he didn't mean to—"

"Of course not. I knew that when it happened. But that's the way his mind works, and we can't budge him."

Helmi had said: we can't go on like this. Now she knew why, and what all the cryptic looks and silences had meant. "That's why the Dumplings didn't attack you here. Doydoy wasn't worth anything to them."

"Yes." Her lips twisted. "We owe our lives to that."

"Can you tell what's happening? Is Jason—"

"Prester, keep still, for God's sake. Yes, he's all right, but I don't envy him. Prothero's so—"

"—damn mad at that peeper I haven't got words for it. Running off when—Waxman, get hold of Casker. I want to talk to that Fitch character." Prothero strode back and forth, cigar in cheekpouch and snarling with the other half of his mouth. The room was blue with smoke, a fair expression of his fuming mood. Urquhart appeared in the doorway with a file folder.

"What the hell do you want?"

Urquhart regarded Prothero with a cold eye. "A civil tongue from you."

Prothero's jaw dropped. He pulled it up again and mumbled, "Sorry, Chris—I can't help—Judas Priest! If I ever live long enough to get my hands on Jason Hemmer—"

There was a noise in the hall, and a second later Jason stepped in. His clothes were rumpled, but his salute was crisp. "Sir?"

Waxman dropped the telephone, but Prothero had been through the whole eight years and was ready for anything. "Damn you, where've you been? Never mind, I'll deal with you later. Get into uniform and start acting like an army man instead of a bloody fool!"

Jason shook his head and said urgently, "Sir, the Dumplings are gone! Right out of range! They were shielding in the woodlot by Craig's Gardens till ten minutes ago, and we —I lost the scramble."

"What! Out of Sorrel Park?"

"Yes. I . . ." He trailed off and stared into space, while Prothero gaped, face purpling, about to explode. "Something's wrong . . . something . . . I . . ."

"What is it, you idiot?"

Jason blinked once and raised his hand to wipe a forehead beaded with sweat "Pres," he whispered. "Come here."

Prester Vernon shot out of the floor like a genie and Waxman's glasses fell off his nose. Jason regarded the apparition with disgust. "Not that way, you ignoramus!" Prester scuffed his feet.

Prothero snarled, "One more trick like that—my God! Casker said there was a new—"

"Yeah. He was telling you the truth. Pres, what's wrong here?"

"That man, Mar—Mar—"

"Marczinek's gone!"

"You're off your head! He was in this room fifteen minutes ago!" Prothero grabbed a phone and rammed a button with his thumb. "Marsh!" he bellowed. "Marsh! Waxman, put a detail on this."

"You won't get an answer," said Jason, "and you won't find him around here. They've got him along."

"They could be a thousand miles away by now! Why did they pick on him for a hostage?"

"Not a hostage. They need an information bank to take the place of Doydoy."

"Damnation, I don't know where to . . ."

Prester closed his eyes and murmured, "They been here, I can feel 'em. But I don't know their thought pattern well enough to follow . . . if Doydoy . . ."

Prothero howled, "You better follow! You damn well better! If you peepers haven't got anything for me in five minutes I'm alerting every popgun within five hundred miles of here!"

"If Doydoy . . ." Helmi whispered. Almost blindly she made her way to Doydoy's room. Shandy followed and watched as she leaned over the bed and shook the still figure. Doydoy twitched under her hand and hunched deeper under the covers.

Helmi shrugged and went to draw the heavy dark curtains and raise the blinds. A dull cold light was filtering past a thin cloud layer. At the touch of the light on his sensitive skin Doydoy reached out a hand and pulled the covers over his head. Shandy knelt beside the bed and gently turned the covers down. His eyes opened a crack, widened an eighth of an inch at the sight of her, and closed once more. His hand

rose to cover his face. Slowly and carefully, Shandy pulled
it away, and ran her fingers over the callused palm. "Why
doesn't he fly instead of crawling on his hands?"

"He's paralyzed: he has no natural sphincter control.
He needs most of his strength to keep himself clean."

"Donatus . . ." The eyes opened again at the unfamiliar
name. She looked up at Helmi and asked timidly, "May I
talk to him?"

"You can try," said Helmi. "A few—maybe five minutes."

"Donatus!" She clutched his hand with wire-tight fingers
so he couldn't free it without stirring enough to open his
mind. "It isn't your fault the Kingfish is dead!"

"Lea-leave me alone," he muttered.

"I can't leave you alone. We need you!"

He tried to pull his hand away. His eyes were still tightly
shut.

"Nobody's blaming you for what happened."

"I'm afraid that argument's worn out," said Helmi.

Doydoy said, half-sobbing, "I to-told you I'm d-angerous.
Da-damn you! Lea' me alone!"

Helmi whispered, "Marczinek! Shandy, they've taken
Marczinek!"

Shandy pulled frantically at Doydoy's wrist. It was muscular and beautifully formed. The surprising power of his
thick arms had always been hidden by the slope of his
shoulders under the hump. "Do you hear that? They've got
Marczinek! He's a gentle old man and they'll kill him!"

Doydoy shuddered and his eyelids squeezed tighter. She
said very urgently and very softly, "It's not shameful to be
afraid of them."

He pulled his spirit further, if possible, into its twisted
shell.

"You've hated them so terribly for eight years—"

His eyes opened wide and closed again.

"Donatus. Are you afraid it wasn't an accident?"

His shoulders shook. "Go away! Go away!"

She squatted back on her heels and looked at the silent
woman by the window. Helmi's lips moved soundlessly: two
minutes.

Nevertheless, she took a precious fifteen seconds to think.
And she said slowly, "They must know you pretty well after
eight years . . . they must have peeped you down to the bottom of the id in the five seconds after you came out of the
cage yesterday. They know you meant to scatter them. They

knew how much you hated them. But they couldn't have known what would happen with those tractors, because you didn't. If they'd had one flicker of an idea you meant to hurt or kill any of them, they'd have shot you down in flames before you'd gone three feet."

She waited tensely for ten seconds. Doydoy's body began to tremble with dry sobs. "They know-know I'm a goddamn cow-ward!"

"No. You're no coward. I'm not saying it's a good idea to kill anybody, either, even a type like the Kingfish. But it *was* an accident, and . . . Donatus, it would have been really horrible if it'd been Curtis Quimper . . . I'm sorry, Helmi." Out of the corner of her eye she had seen the woman stiffen in her attitude by the window.

"It—it's all right . . . you have twenty seconds left before Prothero blows up."

Shandy turned back to Doydoy. "It's all yours now, kiddo. That's it."

Doydoy licked his lips. "They-they'll put me b-ack in the Du-Du-Dump."

"No they won't, said Shandy. "I swear it.. Not any more."

Jason crossed his arms and leaned against the desk as though he had all the time in the world. "It's not use. We just can't pull off this kind of job without Doydoy."

The veins were standing out on Prothero's forehead. "What are you talking about? He's *with* them."

"He is and he isn't. Psychologically, I mean. Physically he's been with us ever since he came out of the cage. That's why I left. To get him away from them—not to go in with them."

"That's what she—the Johnson girl—said after—"

"And you didn't believe her. I know."

"I thought—" Prothero gnawed his lip.

"No. If I'd been with them it wouldn't have been of my own free will . . ." He paused and added delicately, "You could have believed her. I can't read her but I've never known her to lie."

"All of five days."

"You've known *me* four years."

"Damn you, don't read my mind!"

"I can't help it," said Jason.

Prothero breathed hard. "What about Doydoy?"

"He's been curled up in a ball from guilt over killing the

Kingfish. He won't send or receive or even move." He added bitterly, "He's completely harmless."

"What do you mean about his being with them psychologically?"

"You can't blame him if some of his sympathies are with them. Who else ever needed him?" He paused for a moment. "He might be able to trail them for us if we could give him a good reason to help us."

"What kind of reason can you dig up after eight years?"

"He's the only one who can tell what's going on inside a thing or a person . . . all those times I went in and got beaten up . . . all that stuff about broken bones and twisted innards came from him."

"He told you?"

"He could have shielded . . . he left his mind open— because he trusted me." Jason watched Prothero as narrowly as if all his talent and all he knew of the brain-map in the grizzled head were not enough to read him now. "But I couldn't think of trying to get him to help if he was only going to be shoved in the Dump again."

Prothero's face crinkled in suffused fury. "You trying to bargain with me, peeper?"

"Steve!" Urquhart cried. "You've forgotten Marczinek!"

"I haven't forgotten," Prothero growled. "All these years? You!" he shouted at Jason. "Who do you think you are, eighteen years old and giving me orders?" .

Jason's face flamed and darkened the faint traces of his bruises. He opened his mouth to speak, changed his mind and shut up.

Prothero jammed his cigar butt in the ashtray and sparks went flying. "Things will be handled my way or no way. If you can't handle 'em, get out! And you!" He jabbed a finger at Prester, who blinked. "You can—you . . ." His voice broke and his furious color ebbed. "I never thought of it," he whispered. "You're a Negro! There never were any at the plant! We wouldn't take any out of the jail—because the black skin . . . absorbs radiation . . . too . . . my God!"

They stared at Prester. Jason said, "Pres! You never—"

"Quick, boy!" Prothero barked. "Where're you from?"

"I was born here," Prester muttered. "My daddy moved in from Detroit the year of the Blowup when he was kid but he didn't have psi. My granddaddy—on my mother's side—came from Nigeria in '84."

Prothero rammed hands in pockets and paced the floor.

"Is there a reactor in Nigeria? No time to find out now—but if there is—or was, and it skipped a generation! My God!"

Critical mass: thirty-four to begin with, forty-five in the present strength of the Pack without Doydoy . . . *how many Dumps in the world?*

Prothero's shoulders slumped. He said in an achingly weary voice, "Go on. If you can get Doydoy, bring him in."

Jason closed his eyes. Prothero found his handkerchief and swabbed at the erosive wrinkles of his face and neck. Waxman's teeth were chattering. He had only been in Sorrel Park for two months.

Seconds passed and passed; faintly, the air began to tremble; it swirled around them, wavered, wrinkled, and broke like silver water.

Doydoy landed crumpled on the carpet, shivering and gasping.

Jason knelt beside him. "You okay?" Doydoy nodded weakly.

"Pajamas, for God's sake! Tapley, get this man a set of clean fatigues!"

Shandy touched the empty bed, still warm from his body, and collapsed against it, shaking with reactive chill.

sunburst: 12

"THAT BUSINESS with Prester . . ." Shandy pulled herself up wearily. "Every country with its own Dump and Pack?"

Helmi stared out at the desolate street. "I hope not! I don't even want to think of it!"

"What's happening now?" Shandy asked.

"I don't know . . ." She pressed a hand to her forehead. "They're in the Dump, I guess. I can't even get a scrambler."

Peter spoke from the doorway, "I think you are not feeling well."

"I feel all right. It's just . . . I'm alone." At the intensity of the silence behind her, she turned. "I didn't mean anything by that, Peter. I know . . . I have a hell of a nerve saying it, don't I? when I have you, and the baby coming. But you know how I feel. Peter? You know what I am." Her voice was pleading. "I never misled you."

Shandy went to the front door and looked out through the tiny window at a square of sky. Even being Impervious was no help. Helmi's voice trembled behind her: "You always knew what I was. Peter?"

"I knew. And I accepted it."

"You tried, but—"

"Don't tell me what I have in the depth of my soul! If I say I accept it must be enough!"

She whispered, "Don't make it worse for me. I can't help being what I am."

"I have always thought you were making me a—a—"

"A buffer against the world? It's true, but it's only part of the truth. It's not a bad thing, Peter."

"Fools are made that way."

"Peter . . . I could reach into your brain and make you marvelously, idiotically happy with me . . . then you'd be a fool. Or I could make you miserable. But I've never touched you with psi. And there's never anyone else I've wanted to live with. The others—they're only children."

Peter said bitterly, "And suppose there were another in the world? An older one whom you do not know now?"

128

"I'd be scared silly to have a baby by another psi." Her voice shook with tears. "I'm scared now."

"Please. I love you, Helmi."

"I know. And I wish, I wish you *knew* how I love you."

Shandy wanted to scream. Her emotions were flayed to the bone. Her weariness penetrated to the narrow. Her spirit ached. Helmi came into the hall. "It's all right, Shandy. Come on, I'll make some more coffee and we'll sweat it out together."

But there was no time. As Helmi was bringing the coffee-pot to the table, a noise began to grow downward out of the sky. Peter's eye flickered with fear and he leaped up. Helmi caught at his arm. "Wait, Peter."

"What is it?"

"It's . . . Shandy?"

Shandy echoed, "What is it?"

Helmi said faintly, "Will you go outside, and—and see?"

"She must not—"

"It's all right . . . let her go."

Mystified, Shandy opened the front door. There was some-one standing there whom she knew. It was Davey, an old enemy, fist foolishly raised in the air, about to knock.

"You!" she said.

"Yeah, me." He glowered at her. Behind him she saw a helicopter in the vacant lot across the street, engine still running.

"What do you want?"

"I don't want to have anything to do with you! Prothero sent me to pick you up."

She glanced helplessly at Helmi. Helmi said, "You'll have to go, Shandy."

"I—all right . . . good-bye Helmi, Peter . . ." The door closed. She gave him a guarded look. "What would he want with me?"

He snapped, "Maybe he wants to give you a medal!" Then he sighed. "Look, I'm not trying to trick you or any-thing. I figure we're about even." He preceded her down the steps and turned. "He said he needed you."

She came down slowly and followed him. One of her life's aims was about to be accomplished: she was going to become useful. And she was not at all eager to learn how.

The helicopter rose in the air, the earth fell away eerily below, and she saw Sorrel Park as the little place it was, narrow, bitter, twisted, not even an appreciable part of the world. She squeezed close to the window with her head turned away so that the others should not see the fear in her face. Not of death or the Dumplings; she had faced them. But of coming out into the world for good, becoming an organic part of the humanity she had shrunk from without knowing why. The prospect that had made her retreat from Urquhart's probing; a formless fear, but a real one.

From high in the air she saw the green rim of the world surrounding Sorrel Park; the Outside. It was immense and frightening. She had not been afraid for Sorrel Park when the Dumplings were rampaging there—but now she was afraid for the world.

The helicopter landed in the courtyard by headquarters. As the crewmen jumped out, Davey said to Shandy, "Not you. You wait here."

She waited, gripping her knees with sweating palms. The engine was idling, and the sagging rotors trembled. Urquhart ran out a moment later, with a flustered gait, his thin hair ruffling in the wind. He climbed in.

"Shandy? How are you, are you frightened?"

Not the way he meant. "Not yet."

"Good girl." He sat beside her and took her hands. His palms were as wet as her own. "Kiddo, you're going to have to listen very carefully, because I've a lot to say, and not much time to say it in. We've worked out a set of alternative plans here, and their success will depend mostly on you. Believe me, if we had another Imper . . . do you understand?"

"Yes."

"We'll take all the care we can. I—anyway, in a couple of minutes a crew of three will come in here, and then Jason with Doydoy and Prester. They'll give you the creeps because they're all under hypnosis, they won't know you, and it's no use talking to them. I've blocked off all their psi except what they need to track the Dumplings, and the non-psis mustn't know anything they could give away when you come up against them. That kind of thing can't last very long or we'd have used it on the Dumplings long ago—and they mustn't be disturbed or distracted till it's necessary. You understand that."

She smiled a little. "I won't pester them."

"I know you'll be all right, dear." He gripped her hands tighter. "But the group of you will be alone. And *you'll* be

alone as long as they're in that state. You know what I
mean. There'll be plenty of us coming along behind you,
but in this group you'll be alone. The pilot will be radioing
back all the time, but he won't know what it's all about.

"Now: if you find them within six hours, and they're all
together in a bunch, or at least a majority, as I think they'll
be, you'll have to get as close as possible before they know
you're there. That'll be pretty close, because the psis will be
shielding within an hour of picking up the first weak trace.
Then *you* will judge whether there's enough of them grouped
together to warrant going on with the plan."

"Couldn't we radio back the information and let you
decide?"

"That might draw their attention to us telepathically. We
won't send at all. Of course if they're out in the open they'll
hear the rotors, but you should be able to get within a mile
of them, and there may be enough noise from other traffic
to cover you.

"When you're close, you'll have to alight and disembark
because you won't need the machine any more. Then you
keep close together till you're within sight of them. With
luck, they won't know what's going on, and we'll surprise
them. *Then* if things are okay you'll speak the code-phrase
that will bring your group out of hypnosis—and Jason will
know what to do from there."

"Won't the Dumplings know as well?"

"Jason can use any one of a number of plans designed
to meet any conditions—or the pilot can radio back for
changes. None of them knows exactly what they're going to
do right now. It's the only way we can keep the Dumplings
from forestalling us at every move."

"What happens if we can't find them in six hours or they're
hopelessly scattered?" Shandy asked.

"You use the code-phrase as soon as you realize that—
and it should be fairly early—and we regroup and go ahead
with the next plan. But this is how it stands for the time
being. Have you got it all straight?"

"Yes . . . it's on my head."

"Not all of it, Shandy. Too much . . . I know." He
sighed. "Now: the code—and I repeat it depends on you to
judge when to use it—the code-phrase is: *new insight carries
new delight*. Something you wouldn't be likely to say over
the back fence."

"New insight carries new delight . . . did you choose that?"

He blinked. "No. Jason did. Why?"

"It's out of Margaret Mead." *You look like you forgot to ask yourself what would Margaret Mead have done.* He had answered, *Maybe I'll ask you that one day.* "From a passage I liked very much. He knows I read her books, but I never mentioned that bit to him."

"Well, he can't read your mind," said Urquhart, "but I guess he feels he knows your style." In spite of the time limit he had stressed, he kept sitting there, clutching her hands. "You're sure you've got it straight," he said doubtfully.

"I've got it straight," she said. "I give the word when we're in sight of a reasonable concentration of them, or as soon as I see it's all a flop. *New insight carries new delight.*"

"Yes. Well." He pulled his hands away and fished out a handkerchief to swab his head. And he added in a low voice, "You haven't asked what was going to happen to you after all this."

She shrugged ruefully. "I guess I was afraid to."

He shifted in his seat. "You know we want to take the best possible care of you."

"You want to get the Dumplings back." She grinned. "Gee whiz, don't get guilty. I've made a choice and I'm not running away."

"You'll have to do that, too." He gripped her shoulder. "After you give that code I want you to run like hell to the first police station you can find and stay there till we come for you. Promise?"

"I promise."

"We'll take care of you, I swear it. Now good-bye, Shandy." He jumped out to the ground and was gone.

She leaned back. No-one had as yet wished her luck. She supposed it was because they were depending—and wanted her to depend—on her brains.

A pilot and two crewmen ran across the yard, leaped into the cabin, and took their places without a word. She said nothing. Out of the window she saw Jason running, with Doydoy on his back as he had been yesterday when he flew out of the cage. Prester was close behind them. Their eyes were blank; their bodies, in spite of Jason's burden, moved with fatigueless grace.

Prester climbed in first, Jason handed up Doydoy, and they settled him with three cushions piled to support his legs. When they had found their places, the helicopter rose.

She looked at them. Doydoy's eyes were closed, his glasses had slipped down on his nose, and his hands lay at his sides as though they were as dead as his feet. Prester sat gaping like an idiot boy, hands folded loosely in his lap. Urquhart was right. They gave her the creeps.

Jason most of all. He sat back with his arms folded; his eyes slid back and forth in their sockets. They did not rest on her, though she was in his line of vision; for him she was simply not there. The muscles of his brow twitched and puckered, and when he shifted his shoulders every once in a while the dogtags slid in sweat on his neck.

New insight carries new delight. She also had a power, and as she had expected, it weighed her down. She wanted comfort, but there was none she could ask them to give her.

They were still low in the sky; as soon as Sorrel Park had fallen away behind them, the pilot turned the craft and it seemed as if they were heading back again. She had a moment of panic, but when they swung about in a wide arc she realized they were going to follow the slow course of a widening spiral till they could catch the first trace of the Pack.

So she saw Sorrel Park from east, west, north, south; dirty, crammed, jumbled, spirit defiled by barbed wire, smoke from the coal plant staining the pale sky, narrow river carrying detritus out to a distant watershed. The low spiral widened till the town was blued with haze and almost pretty. She thought wryly: at least we're getting out of Sorrel Park.

The silence within hung like a weight beneath the noisy rotors. None of the psis stirred, and she had time to consider the implications of Prester Vernon's black skin. If his grandfather had been exposed to radiation . . . if Nigeria had a Blowup and a Dump of its own . . . if the Dumplings were not found soon . . .

"Go down here."

The voice startled her. It was metallic, toneless, and perfectly articulated—and it was coming from Doydoy.

"Now?" The pilot's voice was equally toneless.

"Yes. A few minutes, please." Shandy was gaping at Doydoy, unable to believe her ears. After a moment, she realized what had happened. Doydoy, reason divorced from emotions under hypnosis, had been freed of his stutter.

The helicopter sank into the middle of an overgrown field, and they waited. No-one moved. Shandy aligned her thoughts as best she could with Doydoy's unimaginable mind: with images in the multifaceted eyes of grasshoppers; with twigs and grasses bruised, stones whose structures had been twisted and distorted, in the wake of the Djinns.

Doydoy opened his eyes and looked around.

The pilot called over his shoulder, "Been here?"

"Yes. Go on."

The pilot sent his message to HQ and they rose and began the new spiral around the X of the field.

Before they had gone round twice Doydoy began to twist in his seat. "He is upset." The metallic voice startled her once again because it was quivering with an amusement he could not have been consciously feeling.

"Who?"

"The farmer. He heard a noise in the chicken-coop and when he went out to look there was nothing left but feathers, bones and heads. It gets him, he says."

"Where is he?"

"On the road two miles west by north, going north with the sheriff in the jeep." The helicopter turned west and the pilot began to murmur over the radio once again.

"He is telling his story over and over. What got him, he says, was the smell of roasting in the air."

The Dumplings were still too civilized to eat raw meat, but they made their own instant cooking arrangements. Five minutes later the helicopter passed over the head of the farmer gesticulating beside the sheriff in the jeep; swung north, found the farm and circled it. And drew its invisible line between field and farm, an arrow pointing out into the world, toward the Dumplings.

"The animals are disturbed," said Doydoy.

Beyond the arrow, the helicopter began to swing back and forth in a widening fan-shaped course. It swung and swung like a cradle suspended from a tree-branch until, though she was not sleepy, she became numb from rhythm, vibration, weariness.

It was noon, a fantastic unreal zenith of the day. The sky was empty.

"Go down here." A cropped field this time; a flock of sheep scattered bleating for the fence-rails. They had not been eaten—perhaps they had narrowly escaped being slaughtered for fun. "Northwest now." The incorporated mind drew a new arrow-line between farm and field; again they rose and began a splayed course outward.

At the peak of the third pendulum-swing, Doydoy cried out. "It's terrible!" There was no amusement in his voice.

The pilot turned. "What?"

"The pain."

"Huh?"

"Woman . . . left for dead by the roadside. Three miles north of Pineville, Highway 18."

Shandy pressed her face to the window; a crumpled shape half-hidden by leaves was down there by the side of the road. But they would not stop. She began to tremble. She wanted to yell *Stop!* There was life down there, ebbing. She felt the pain and the warm wet of the blood seeping in the pebbled earth, and memories enough to drive one mad. *New insight carries new delight.* She crammed the knuckles of her forefingers in her mouth and bit down. She was alone.

The course was now a straight one, due north. Doydoy said, "We are shielding." Shandy glanced at the watch on Jason's wrist. Four hours more for the limit in which she must speak the phrase. *Left for dead by the roadside,* she thought bitterly, would not wake them.

There was no escape. The course ran north, eating miles, and a blue line threaded itself across the horizon. It looked like the boundless sea to Shandy, but she knew it was Lake Michigan, and the smoky blur before it, Chicago.

In a brief fantasy she saw the helicopter landing and stopping, herself jumping out without a word to the blind blank figures beside her, and losing herself in the great city, out in the world and free. But she was in no more danger of doing that than of being able to fly like Doydoy.

The countryside thickened with houses and gas stations, planes appeared overhead, noise drowned out by their own; further away, gnatswarms of hovercraft were buzzing over the city. The distant haze resolved itself, not smoke as it would have been in Sorrel Park, but the mist of a lakeside city steaming in a drizzling June day.

The mist thinned on approach; towers still unbroken rose like marvels, a million windows flickering against the pale sky. She had imagined them, but had never expected to know them, and she reveled in them. The Pack was loose, the woman was bleeding by the roadside, and she was merely happy to be alive.

There were no visible scars on the surface of the city. It extended itself beneath them in squares, segments, triangles, rhombuses, parallelograms, and the traffic moved in a metallic many-celled stream from narrow streets into twisting knotted entries to multiple-laned freeways furious with urgency and complex as the vascular tree. White lights glared in the dull day from every shaft of glass and steel. The upper air quivered with its own traffic, and on distant fields there were ships rising beyond the air.

Within a mile there were forty-five people who could destroy it all with wish.

They moved forward slowly. She looked down; something was happening to the surge of mid-day traffic. It was beginning to ebb, with much snarling and clogging, from the crowded center. Small black-and-white saucer-shaped police-copters were buzzing over intersections, leading automobiles and buses away from the center. Storm-warnings were up.

"Right there," Doydoy said.

"That's the Loop."

"No. South. The computers."

The pilot whistled, impressed even under hypnosis. "The Chicago Pentagon!"

Now Doydoy began to twitch and thresh in his seat, caught in an unconscious terror. Shandy watched helplessly. But the pilot was calm. He circled in a slow downward spiral, like a gull wheeling toward the sea. Doydoy's legs had slid from the pile of cushions; Jason and Prester were still and gaping beside him, but he clawed at the air in an extremity of fear; sweat broke out on him so sharp and sudden the splotches flared on his shirt like spattered raindrops. He twitched and stuttered, "Com-Com-munica-cations Cen-Cen-Center in-in Depar-par-par—"

"Department of Strategic Services!" the pilot yelled. "Right!"

Shandy pressed her face to the downslanting window and saw a remarkably insignificant office building surrounded by a great swathe of grass dotted with flowerbeds. The buzzing craft around them had withdrawn; the sky was empty.

And Doydoy began to wail. The sound was terrifying; the power of his fear of the Dumplings was something no hypnosis could control.

The grounds below were deserted. Shandy pulled at Jason's arm. "Quick! Are they down there? Are they all there?"

Jason blinked. "Yes, I—"

Above them, with a savage rip, the rotors broke off and flew to the four winds; the helicopter plunged out of the sky. Shandy, trying frantically to force the code-phrase between her lips, found her throat torn open in an endless scream.

sunburst: 13

"—CARRIES NEW DELIGHT! Oh my God, new insight carries—"

She had not lost consciousness, but the jolting change from one second to the next gave the same impression. She was crouched on the floor with her fingers locked in a plexus over her skull to protect the vulnerable bones.

"It's okay." Jason was on his feet beside her, wide-eyed and alert. Prester was pulling up Doydoy, who had slid to the floor and was trying to put on his glasses. One of the lenses was cracked.

She sat up. Things did not look okay to her. The pilot was sprawled unconsicious over the instrument panel, a thin line of blood running down his temple, and the crewmen, dazed, were pulling themselves up off the floor. But the psis were no longer under hypnosis. Either the code-phrase or the shock of falling—she didn't want to know which—had brought them to their senses. The helicopter, minus rotors, was still in the air. As she was absorbing the shock of this discovery, it gently lowered itself a couple of feet, and grounded.

Jason glanced at her in passing. "You look all right." He told the crewmen, who were bending over the pilot, "He's just knocked out. Grab his arms and we'll get you out of this. You can find a hospital. Understand?" One of them nodded dazedly. "Don't be scared. Go on, Pres."

Prester snapped his fingers and the men disappeared.

"Him!" Jason snorted. "Gotta have a gesture for everything. Shandy, you get out and run like hell!"

The door opened. She leaped out, but her legs buckled under her. Jason jumped down beside her and grabbed her elbow. "Come on, you got to . . . Jeez, now we got the whole city on us." Crowds were converging from the rim of the green lawn. "Get rid of them, Pres—no fireworks," and the running figures turned and began to race back the way they had come, trampling each other in their haste.

The helicopter burst into flames. "Get going, Shandy!" Jason gave her a push that sent her flying, and she rolled

137

out of the way with a speed and energy that surprised her. Then the burning helicopter disappeared, and Prester, carrying Doydoy, ran out from the scorched area it had occupied. He was swearing intensely in a style far beyond his years. He set Doydoy on the grass and murmured, "Somebody playing keepsies."

Doydoy pointed at the building and squeaked, "J-Jocko, in-inside!"

"Yeah, the lookout." Jason chewed his lip. "They're underground."

Shandy asked, "The building isn't all?"

"Heck, no. Just administration. Underground they got computers. A lead-and-steel maze a mile deep and a mile square. If they tried to teep from there they might end up inside a wall. That's why they need Jocko here."

"He's knocked out the people upstairs," Prester said. "Killed two." He added thoughtfully, "Like to pick off that boy."

"We'll do that," Jason said. ". . . Boy, we sure picked a lousy place to be stuck out in the middle of." They were half-hidden by a flowerbed, but there was a terrible expanse of unsheltered lawn between them and the federal building to the north. "Go on, Shandy, scram!"

She turned and ran without a word. The grass was spongy, and moisture from the recent rains was beginning to seep through the soles of her shoes. The air was humid, but there was only a thin haze of cloud; the sun would shine within an hour, and it seemed unjust that there should be so much terror on a June day in Chicago.

She looked back once. Jason and Prester were pounding in back of her. Doydoy had disappeared, and Jason yelled, "Run! Run!" She ran. After a dozen steps she heard cries behind her and whirled in time to see Jason and Prester struggling with four or five Dumplings. Within a second, they vanished. She dithered a moment. It was impossible to help them now, and she went on with aching legs, knowing that if the Dumplings decided to stop her all the speed she could muster was no use.

She was right. A wall of two Dumplings, shoulder to shoulder, broke out of the air with a crash before her, and she slammed into them. They grasped her each to an arm; she pulled back, struggling. She knew one of them. It was Frankie Slippec, but there was no sign of recognition in his eyes.

Without a word they started pulling her toward the building. She twisted and cried out in their grasp, but it was no use. There was no-one to save her here.

They couldn't pk her, but they were fast. Up stone steps, across the lobby, down halls heaped with senseless bodies, down stairs leaping from landing to landing because elevators were too slow. She collapsed in their grip, half-fainting.

At last only the elevator could take them where they wanted to go. They pushed her in, crammed in after her, and in defiance of controls sent it falling like a meteor down subterranean shafts of lead and steel built to withstand the bomb that had not yet dropped.

After some trial and error they had solved the maze of caverns and tunnels by blazing a trail in scorchmarks on the composition floor; they followed it down twisting byways until a pocket of light at the end, and a growing hum of machines, rewarded them. When they had reached the great chamber of the control room, they stopped and let her go.

Quivering in all her bones, Shandy tried to pull herself together, and screwed up her eyes at the blaze of light from walls and ceiling. This, she understood finally, was what Doydoy had meant, blurting through chattering teeth about communications centers and computers.

The walls were covered with charts, grids, and edge-lit world maps flickering in spectrum colors. Ranged before them were six great consoles studded with controls. The men and women who had handled them had been knocked out and shoved into corners like rag dolls. Marczinek, useless too because he could not run a computer, had been flung into a console chair; his head lolled, his arms hung limp, and his gaudy shirt was bloody.

Jason and Prester were standing near him; all the Dumplings were around them. But Doydoy was gone.

She ran over to Marczinek, but Curtis Quimper said, "Stay where you are. He's alive, and you want to keep him alive."

"But—"

Jason stopped her with an outstretched arm. "Keep out of the way. We can't do anything for him now."

She moved back to the wall. "Where's Doydoy?"

The Dumplings scuffled. Curtis Quimper breathed hard. "Looks like he got away."

"Lost him again! That's good."

"Never mind. We'll get him back."

"I thought you didn't care about him any more."

Jason said, "They think they'll get him to run this thing." He waved a hand to indicate the huge installation.

"What for?"

"Power," said LaVonne. "Know what this controls? The country: telephones, cables, trains, planes, airships, warning systems, rockets, missiles, and—a lot more I forget. The country . . . maybe half the world."

"You don't need Doydoy for that. You could have figured it out from these people here." She nodded at the crumpled shapes in the corner.

"They raised a fuss . . . we didn't think they'd wear too well."

Jason said flatly, "That's a lie. The state they were in when they came down here they were only too happy to knock anybody around." The Pack's fury, frightening as it was, was also its weak point.

"Watch out," said Curtis Quimper.

Shandy observed them narrowly: LaVonne and Curtis Quimper. The Kingfish was dead, and Curtis was weakening and tiring with increased age and the savage use he had made of his abilities. LaVonne could reason on deeper and more hidden levels than the rest, and outmatch any of them. She would know they would never let a girl lead them—much less a girl who was a twisted and ugly dwarf; but she was there to lend Quimper her strength—until the day he became too tired. After him . . . there were thirty-eight other potential leaders.

"I thought you respected the truth quite a lot," said Shandy.

"Stuff that," LaVonne said. "We want Doydoy."

"Thought you were playing it smart," said Curtis. "Give up two little psis so the big one could get away? You didn't figure we'd get your Imper and your plans're shot to hell."

"She has nothing to do with it," Jason said quickly.

"We think she's got a lot to do with it. She's an Imper, ain't she? Nobody knows what's in her head. We'll find out."

Jason moved over and stood in front of Shandy. "Don't try it."

LaVonne snickered. "Lookit the great protector. Little gentleman!" She leered up at him and a raw flush seeped up from his neck and out to the rims of his ears. LaVonne outraged his manhood.

"Listen, you know you'll have to take the two of us"—

he indicated Prester—"before you get her. You don't want to waste even our psi."

"Little man," LaVonne giggled, "you got funny ideas. Think we wouldn't do that to get Doydoy?"

Shandy thought they would. They would risk a lot to get Doydoy because they needed him in more ways than they would admit. Not only for power. He was their memory and their reasoning ability as well. Their memories were so short and their attention span so limited that without him they forgot not only what they had read in his mind but also most of what they had learned for themselves from experience.

She stepped out from behind Jason. "I believe you—but you don't have to do anything. I don't know where Doydoy is."

"I don't believe you!" LaVonne spat. "But I won't have to waste much time breakin' you." The Dumplings began to move in.

But Shandy kept watching LaVonne. The most horrifying thing about her now was that she had so involved herself in evil she was inextricable. There was no appeal to be made to her and nothing worth saving about her.

Without taking her eyes off LaVonne, Shandy said, "I didn't know you'd retired, Curtis."

"What's that?"

She crossed her arms and leaned on the console in back of her. "Looks like you're letting LaVonne take over."

"Take over!" Curtis Quimper sneered. "Who said anything—"

"She's doing most of the talking, isn't she? You know, LaVonne's so strong and smart she can keep any thoughts she likes hidden from you . . . she could even fix things so her left hand didn't know what her right hand was doing, and she's your right hand, Curtis."

"You're nuts!"

"Maybe, but I'm not stupid."

"You just think you're smart," LaVonne said through her teeth.

Shandy ignored her. "Curtis . . . I'm not a psi, but I bet somewhere in a corner of your mind you're tired of this . . . you don't really want to have to fight Jocko, or Colin, or Buttsy, or whoever else gets big ideas—even with LaVonne helping you. I haven't got your kind of power, but I did do a lot to get Doydoy out of the Dump, and he's not going in again whatever happens"—she searched the depthless planes of his eyes—"because he helped us.

"You're burning out. You won't be any use to this bunch soon, and you'll end up dead . . . but you could be a lot of use to us for many years." She thought Jason might stick his neck out for anything at this point. "Help us now and there might be something in it for you."

His glance flicked at Jason, and a play of emotions swept over his face. LaVonne watched him. After a moment, he snorted: "You got some offer there. You're offering to let me help you!"

A waste of breath. But she had shifted their attention for the moment from herself—and Doydoy. "I'm not offering. I'm begging you to help us and save yourself before Prothero gets here and spoils your chance."

LaVonne snapped, "Tell us where Doydoy is before Prothero gets here and maybe we'll leave you alive. Maybe."

"I don't *know* where he is—but I bet he's not far away; I bet he knows what's going on down here—and if I were Doydoy I'd have picked off Jocko while you were shooting off your mouth about what you were going. to do."

LaVonne's face twisted. "Whaddya think you're—" She stopped short and licked her lips. She whispered, "Jocko?"

The Dumplings moved, blinked, turned on small axes and stared at each other. The machines chattered around their silence.

Curtis turned to Shandy. "What's going on here?"

She gasped, "I swear—"

"Read me!" Jason snarled. "She's got no psi. I monitored all her—"

But Curtis Quimper had no more time to waste on them. "Somebody's gotta get up there! Fast!"

One of the Dumplings tp'd to the doorway. "Trail's gone!"

"Gone! Somebody hiding something here?"

"It wasn't any of us, Quimp, honest!"

Curtis was breathing hard. "Get up there! Any way! Burn a hole, but get up there! You, Nick! You hear me?"

"Me? Awright, I'm going." He backed out of the door. "Okay, o—"

Silence.

"Nick?"

"Nick! Where is he? Now what'n hell's going on here!"

"I got him! He—no, he's lost!"

"Nick?"

"He's fadin' out! He—"

"Lost! Goddamn, he just went outa this door! How—" Curtis Quimper swung round to face Jason. "Somebody's, playing, games."

"Not us, Quimp." Jason's mouth barely twitched with a smile. "This is somebody with real power."

"Doydoy? Hey, Doydoy!"

"Come on, Nick!"

"—and he—he's scared, he—"

"Lead and steel," said Jason. "That's the beauty of it. Too bad we couldn't have done that with the Dump."

"You talk too much," said LaVonne. Jason slumped to the floor. Shandy screamed and dropped to her knees beside him.

Prester said quickly, "Leave him. It's a pinched carotid, he'll only be out a couple minutes."

Marczinek. Jason. Shandy's glance flicked from one to the other. Every breath spread the stain of blood on Marczinek's shirt; Jason's face was white and sick. They were helpless. But she was not. If Doydoy were really anywhere near . . .

She pulled over very slightly toward Prester and whispered, "Shield." His eyelids twitched.

Somebody yelled, "What're we gonna do now? You got us into this!"

"Yeah! Jocko's gone, Nick—"

"—ain't gone, they're—"

"—screaming! Goddam walls!"

They looked at each other. Sweat beaded their faces.

LaVonne planted hands on hips and scoured them with contempt. "Scared, babies? Wantcher didies changed?"

Curtis poked her. "Shut up, Pigface!"

She had cringed at the name before it reached his lips. Her eyes slitted. "Gee, Quimp, you looked like you were punkin' out. I thought you needed a little help."

"I can ask for it." He faced the Pack, glaring. They shuffled their feet and he reinforced the message: "Stick together, keep 'em scared. Bust out, we can run into a bomb. You want it? Okay!"

Shandy had crawled back, inching, till she was half-hidden by a console. Prester moved over slightly, still in view, but at watch and shielding. She whispered, "Can Doydoy shield and still read you?" His nod was almost imperceptible.

"Can you open up to him without their knowing?" Nod. "Listen: you're no more use here. I'll give them something to think about, and I want Doydoy to get you and Jason and Marsh out."

Before he could protest she began to crawl, as slowly as if she meant it, past the console, toward the shelter of the next one, and beyond it, the door. Prester plucked at the leg of her jeans, but she pulled away. She did not expect to get far. The composition floor, flecked with gold and pearl, was cool and smooth under her hands. Pawn to King four, she crossed the square lines. To the shadow of the next console . . .

"Look what we got here!"

The pop of tp and two feet planted before her at the edges of her fingernails. She looked up. Curtis Quimper was regarding her with amusement. She thought of Helmi, and of the woman by the road near Pineville, and her mouth went dry.

He pulled her up by the neck of her jersey. Beyond the laughter of the Djinns rebounding from the walls, beyond the helpless fear, she saw that his skin was as dark, his hair as black, his eyes as blue as her own.

"Talk about punkin' out?" His mouth was tight. He pushed her back at the end of his arm and pinned her with a hand against the console. The Pack moved in, waiting. They had forgotten their fear, and she had not many hopes left for Curtis Quimper. She kicked, clawed, twisted. *Now Prester,* she begged silently.

Curtis laughed. "Lookit the bug on the pin," he said. "How far did *you* expect to get?"

A small explosion broke the air behind them. They whirled.

Shandy stopped struggling. "There it is." Marczinek's chair was empty, Jason and Prester were gone. The unconscious bodies in the corner had disappeared. The Dumplings gaped. "That's just as far as I hoped to get," she said, and closed her eyes.

There was a roar. Hands grasped and threw her; hands caught, tossed, caught. The breath drove out of her chest, her hair broke free and swirled, the shoes flew off her feet. She opened her eyes as her hair swept the soundproof tile of the ceiling, and fell in a soundless scream to be caught, tossed, skimming a console-top, caught half an inch short of the wall; eyelids fluttering in nerveless blink caught light off now bared savage teeth, now flickering dial, now eyewhites;

spreadeagled on the floor foot planted against ribs ready to crush, and gibbering, baying—

"STOP IT!" It was Curtis Quimper. From habit they stopped; the foot rose. Flat on the floor, eyes closed, she lay half-dead.

"—the hell you—"

"—for Chri—"

"—gone soft in the nut?"

She forced her eyes open a slit, and a frieze of legs flickered before them.

Curtis howled, "You mutts, we got no more hostages!"

LaVonne laughed, a hoarse, ugly bark. *"You* got no more hostages!" As her voice thinned in a scream at the last word, Curtis rose in the air, twisted in a tight arc, landed on his shoulder with a crunch of bone, and lay still.

LaVonne screeched, "Now you listen to me!" But Frankie Slippec turned on her.

"I had enough of your snot!" He ran for the door.

She looked at him. He stopped in mid-leap, shivered, and collapsed.

"Dead . . ." They trembled with his pain, and were quiet. They had committed obscenities, they had killed, but always, within their own distorted code, on fair terms. This was different.

"Now will you listen!"

They waited. LaVonne raised her head and screamed at the ceiling. "Doydoy! Doydoy! You hear me, Doydoy, it's your last chance! You come down here and get us out or I break this place. Hear me? I'll break it! You know what that means, Doydoy? You come down here!"

They knew what it meant. The communications and controls of the whole country and half the world.

Silence. Around the center of silence the machine racketed on.

"Is that . . ."

"He's—"

"Here?"

A presence whispered around them. Shandy, astonished, felt it. A power so strong it found response even in her unresonating mind. Doydoy?

"There he is!" A group clubbed itself together at one side of the room, suddenly. "Come on!"

"What're you talkin' about?" LaVonne gaped at them.

"He's down the hall!"

"No he ain't, he's—"

"There he is, I see him! Doydoy!" Ten Dumplings vanished.

LaVonne screeched after them, "You boobs, he's tricking you, he's—"

They became still, turned, listened. Buttsy whispered, "He's upstairs." Ricci, Gloria, Lenny moved over beside him, faces upturned.

Doydoy appeared, hovered beneath the ceiling, blinked once, and disappeared. Buttsy's group shouted and vanished with him.

"It's not him!" LaVonne hissed. "It's not him, he's faking a—"

"This *is* me." They wheeled. Doydoy was crouched against the slanted deck of one of the console tables. He was no longer afraid of Dumplings. He smiled like a Cheshire cat, rose in the air, and vanished through the door to the scanning room.

Before they could follow, LaVonne called, "Wait!" She ran over to where Shandy was lying half-dazed with pain and began to tug at her. "It's our hostage. Come on, help me." She and Colin Prothero got her up and, half-dragging, half-stumbling, pulled her along with them. Through the silent library, memory stores, scanning rooms where machines spun reels of microfilm and glared at flicking pages through lenses, their steps scuffled and scattered.

There was nothing there. Even the sense of his presence had died.

They whispered, "He's gone." They pushed further, gasping for breath, glazed with fear, in rooms where components were stored, books, papers, small machines rattling to themselves. To the end. Blank walls of steel.

LaVonne, sobbing, streaming with sweat, cried, "Go on!" A wall melted, lead beyond. "Go on!" LaVonne screamed. Lead quivered like jelly and ran down to their feet, hissing and slopping. "Go on!" Holes, cracks, fissures grew. Rock beyond.

"There's nothing! Where's the others?"

". . . alone . . . nothing."

"I say he's here! He's here!" They stared at her and began to back away. She breathed hard. "I tell you, he—" But there was nothing she could tell them. They scattered through doors, walls, columns of air.

LaVonne, still clutching Shandy, wept. Colin was the only

one left with her. He had not had the courage to leave.

"Doydoy . . . he did it," she sobbed. "That little bastard . . ."

He had not even brought them to the surface to rage or scatter before they could be netted. He had merely deployed them in the labyrinth, lost without co-ordinates or links to the outside, to beat against the heavy shielding walls, to scream loneliness and fear to every other member of the Pack, to melt a wall of lead and steel and find more walls beyond.

Every time they had given in to their careless fury he had taken another and another. Doydoy, the only gentle one, the most powerful, and the one who most hated power, was teaching them the only lesson they could be taught.

LaVonne panted, "I'm not finished. I can do something, too."

"Don't," Colin whispered. "Don't do that."

"You want—what Frankie got! That's what you—"

"No, no, LaVonne, don't!"

"Then get going!"

"Let's leave her here, at least."

"We'll leave her in the middle of it! Now come on!"

Shandy's feeble struggles were no match for the power of fury and despair. They pushed, shoved, dragged her, panting and sobbing, back to the control room. Curtis lay alone there, unconscious. The machine paid them no heed. It chuffed and chattered hugely in emptiness.

LaVonne swung her Medusa head. "Now!"

Colin cried, "No! No!"

LaVonne smiled evilly. "I don't need you." He fell.

Shandy, without his support, found her legs buckling, and she slid down beside him.

From the floor, eyes glazing, too far gone for horror, she watched as LaVonne clenched her fists and spun like a gyroscope. Bells rang, lights flashed, the air quivered with hoots and whistles. LaVonne, gasping, raised her arms, clawed air with her fingers, eyes turned back in the sockets till the blind whites stared; alarms hooted around her, maps broke on the walls, sirens screamed, consoles split and crashed to the floor in a white heat and sank in puddled tiles. Shandy felt the scorch through her clothes, tried to pull herself up and fell back. Dials snapped, racks shattered, walls of panels trembled, rippled, and dropped in molten rains. The machine and its world died in fury around them.

LaVonne howled, a coyote's empty triumph. Her eyes lowered and found Shandy.

"You," she whispered. "You did it too. Now you." She tottered over and reached down.

The hands groped for her neck, and Shandy stirred feebly, without hope. She thought, with a deeply private agony: *Now I'll never find out.*

About herself; about everything in the world. Everything.

Behind LaVonne, someone moved. Curtis Quimper, groaning in pain, reached out and pulled at her leg. She turned to kick him away.

Something fell into the room, hissing. She looked up. A metal cylinder, with a thin vapor flaring from it. She blinked in a daze, took two wobbling steps, and fell.

No Dumplings, no machine broke silence. Only the stream of gas hissing from the bomb.

Shandy knew one more thing before she went down into the blackness. A towering, bulky-suited figure waded into the room and began to search through the wreckage. Through the bubble-helmet she recognized Prothero. He found what he was looking for at her feet and bent over the body of his son, face scarred with the marks of his bitter, helpless love.

sunburst: 14

ONCE SHE WOKE in the dark. She saw lamplight through slitted lids and shapes moving before it. Her mouth was dry and she moved her head back and forth, unable to speak. A hand steadied her, a glass tube was offered at her lips; she drank.

A voice rumbled, "How is she?" Prothero.

Urquhart's voice said, "She'll be all right."

A cool hand trembled on her forehead. "I don't want you wearing her out." Grace Halsey.

He said with asperity, "I'm just as concerned as you are. I intend to be careful."

Shandy unlimbered her tongue along the roof of her mouth and licked her lips. "Marczinek," she whispered.

"He's badly hurt," said Grace, "but alive. Go to sleep, dear."

She croaked, "The machine—LaVonne—"

Urquhart said, "The computer's ruined, but there were three other peer machines over the country taking over right away—it's lucky we were too shut in here to know about them—and we've got LaVonne in the cage. The world's still running, and you can get to sleep."

"Jason—"

"They're all safe," Grace said. "That's enough talk for now."

A needle pricked her arm and she slipped into a darkness where she battled screaming nightmares and floundered in seas of terror for days, until at last she washed up on a bank of silence.

Urquhart: Shandy. Can you hear me?
Shandy: Yes. Am I dreaming?
Urquhart: No. Open your eyes. Can you see me?
Shandy: Yes.
Urquhart: Good. Do you feel well?
Shandy: I'm aching all over. What do you want?
Urquhart: I want to talk to you for a while.

Shandy: You—have you hypnotized me? I feel strange.

Urquhart: No, I haven't hypnotized you. But there're things I want to find out. I'm not going to try any depth analysis, but I told you I wanted to know how you tick . . . I've just given you drugs to relax you a little and release some of your inhibitions.

Jason: Inhibitions! Did she ever have any?

Shandy: If I've got no inhibitions I can tell you what I think of you, you big ape!

Jason: She sounds like herself.

Urquhart: Jason, I think you have a right to be here, but if you're going to make a fuss you can get out.

Jason: Okay, okay.

Urquhart: Shandy, Jason's been telling me about your idea . . . about psi, and about the delinquent's being the victim of genetic defect.

Shandy: I didn't mean it for anything definite. It was just one way of putting things together.

Urquhart: I understand that. Whether it'll hold water is something else again, but I'd like to hear a little more about it.

Shandy: I don't think there's much to say about it. Just —if you look at delinquents, and at the Dumplings, they seem to separate themselves into a distinct physical and emotional type. I don't know what happens with Negroids and Mongolians—

Urquhart: Oh, I'll promise not to use them for an arguing point right now. What's the basis for your conclusions?

Shandy: Well, first of all, distinct behavior patterns turn up in them even when they're little kids. They're restless and active, and wet their beds till they're quite big. By the time they're fourteen they've probably been in trouble with the police several times already . . . and instead of feeling guilty they just feel everybody's against them. They're generally mesomorphic, and kind of runty till puberty, and then they grow up suddenly; and they keep on being hostile, suspicious and defiant, and can't put off anything they want at the moment, or make plans for the future . . .

Urquhart: And they often have the brainwaves of children —and also immature patterns of capillary loops in their fingertips—

Shandy: Do they? I didn't know that.

Urquhart: But it's no real excuse for calling them animals.

Shandy: No, but it is a physical thing that separates them

from other people. I've heard there've been lots of hopeless psychopaths with normal brainwaves—but I don't think they'd have been Dumplings. I guess the most animal thing about them is that they have to have everything for today. And the hostility.

Urquhart: A lot of them calm down in their thirties.

Shandy: So do the lions in the zoo when they lose their teeth—and for these people the whole world is a zoo. I know it'd be hard to pick them out of the ordinary criminal lot till they've made themselves and everybody else so miserable they can't be helped. I'd even be sorry if anybody found an absolutely definite way of identifying them because then you'd have some crank yacking that they ought to be sterilized, and that'd be awful. I don't know what ought to be done for them—but I think there ought to be better ways to weed them out and handle them when they're young and dangerous—without being either cruel or soppy—until they're fit to live in society, and I think this idea might help people look at them more calmly.

Urquhart: Um. All right. Now the other thing. People have had some pretty wild romantic dreams about psi over the ages. I'll admit the Dumplings aren't anybody's dream of Superman come true. But you seem to feel it's—"garbage" was the term you used.

Shandy: Yes, because the creatures that have it all turn out to be primitive. Pk and tp are just extra physical power, and telepathy is a way of communicating if you don't have speech. The way telepathy turns up in animals it's probably pretty clumsy. For herd animals that have to stick together it might be useful, but I bet a human being born with it could never separate his mind from everybody else's long enough to develop a logical idea.

Urquhart: Jason, Prester, Helmi and Doydoy don't fit your definition of animals, and they have psi.

Shandy: I can't explain them. I'm just glad they're here.

Urquhart: . . . And you say the Dumplings became psis because radiation would do more harm, produce a more bizarre effect, on the gonads of parents who would be likely to have defective children anyway.

Shandy: Yes.

Urquhart: And psi is definitely not the attribute of the supernormal?

Shandy: Gee whiz, you sound so disappointed! Maybe one day . . . but I think it'd be a long time before people could bear knowing each other's miseries telepathically—and what would scientists and artists do if they couldn't be alone to think? Real super-psis would be too much of a jump away from us, and evolution works slowly.

Urquhart: Then how would you picture a supernormal who seemed reasonable in relation to Homo sapiens?

Shandy: I never thought about that. Do I have to? I'm sleepy . . .

Urquhart: Take a stab at it. You don't have to knock yourself out.

Shandy: I—I don't know . . . I guess you start with brains.

Urquhart: It's the classic gambit.

Shandy: Well, I don't think the world'd get much use out of a super-kook. But . . . there's been lots of geniuses in the world, and many of them have been unhappy . . . and a lot of them have been nasty.

Urquhart: Superman has to be noble.

Shandy: Not goody-goody. But he has to be moral or he'll do harm. Even the brightest kid gets pushed around by all sorts of things while he's growing up, and you can't always be sure he'll turn out moral.

Urquhart: You want a person who's protected from the mischances of psychodynamic forces.

Shandy: Yes. Somebody who'd turn out to be moral no matter what happened to him.

Urquhart: Stable moral equilibrium.

Shandy: With plenty of room to be different. Otherwise, supernormals would be dull—and I don't think they'd last. Suppose he started off with a lot of the best building materials—and arranged them however he liked, or however life pushed them around for him. But whatever he started with, however it got arranged in a million possible ways, he'd end up with something balanced. Even if it didn't look like much, even if it looked kind of loony from the outside.

Urquhart: If it looked too crazy he'd never be respected . . .

Shandy: Some might get lost . . . but that's the chance he'd have to take in the evolutionary battle, like everybody else under the sun.

Urquhart: Your superman's vague.

Shandy: If he looked too beautiful or noble or eccentric he might be picked out and pushed aside. You'd want him to be an organic part of humanity, to give his qualities to his children—if he could transmit them. I can't think of anybody like that as other-directed, so I guess he'd keep out of the way and stay inconspicuous till his building materials were permanently arranged. And he'd watch and learn and wait.

Urquhart: Wait for what?

Shandy: To find out what he was.

Urquhart: Why would he have to find out?

Shandy: Because a bright person who isn't curious is useless. There's plenty of decent lumps in the world, but they can't stand a new idea, and they're more harm than help. He'd have to find out what he was because he couldn't help finding out everything he could.

Urquhart: And after he found out?

Shandy: He'd try to find a place for himself in society, and get married, I guess, and have his kids.

Urquhart: It's a modest superman.

Shandy: He's a kind ordinary people could live with, even if they felt he was a little eccentric. He'd have the same emotions and the same hopes. That's why I think he'd have a chance. You couldn't expect an advance to come in a single impossible leap to the summit. One step would be enough.

Urquhart: Would he be happy?

Shandy: His life might be hard and lonely, he might wish he weren't different at all—but I don't see how he could be really unhappy when he had the whole universe to observe and learn about and understand.

Urquhart: I see. One more thing, Shandy. What kind of child do you think your superman would have been?

Shandy: Child? Gee, I dunno . . . I don't think I ever knew or heard of a bright kid who wasn't something of a nudnik, so I guess he'd be that . . . and . . . and he'd have to stay a kid a long time to build that kind of complicated moral structure in himself . . .

Urquhart: Yes . . . I think so. Anybody you know . . . who fits that description?

Shandy: . . . I . . . I don't—I—Oh . . .

Grace: She's upset. Now look what you've done!

Urquhart: It's all right . . . Helmi, Prester, Jason—they've managed with psi. She can manage with this. Come on, Shandy, calm down. You'll get used to it.

She woke to an afternoon light coming through the window. She was in her old room, and the first thing she noticed was that the broken panes had been replaced. And the next, that her bed had bars.

She crawled over them clumsily, blinked away a wave of

dizziness, and found she was wearing a coarse white hospital gown. She tottered over to the window and rested her hands on the sill. It was warm from the sun. Someone was singing below; not Marczinek; a baritone:

Gonna hoe corn, drink it till I die . . .

She pushed up the screen and put her head out the window, elbows on the sill. Jason had dug up Marczinek's flowerbed, and was shoveling on loam from a wheelbarrow. He looked up and grinned, presumably at her expression.

"What do you expect to plant this late in the season?"

"Hollyhocks," he said happily, "hardy phlox, four-o'clocks, and Urquhart's coming down the hall."

She pulled back hastily and jumped into bed. Jason kept singing:

Gonna hoe that corn, keep drinkin' till I die,
Singin' the workshirt blues 'cause I'm too old to cry . . .

Urquhart wandered in and sat on the bed. "You look beat, but I'm told you'll be all right. Hungry?"

"Not yet. What's today?"

"Wednesday."

"What have I missed?"

He grinned. "Nothing you couldn't do without."

"I'm scared to ask . . . how Marczinek is."

He shrugged. "He's an old man . . . and they weren't gentle."

"I—I know Frankie Slippec's dead, and—and Colin . . . LaVonne was trying to make as much mess as she could."

"She did plenty. Buttsy, Willy, Gloria—they're dead, and the rest got banged up in varying degrees, but they'll live."

Curtis was alive then—and Doydoy. "I still can't understand how it ended as it did. It seemed impossible for them to lose."

He shook his head. "No, Shandy. They made it impossible for themselves to win. It's true they made a big mess—but look at the record. First, they picked Marczinek only because he knew there was an important computer in Chicago. He couldn't run one, he had no psi, and he didn't know that five or six years ago equally important connecting centers were set up in San Francisco, Edmonton, and Boston. As soon as they got the wind up, the government shifted the Chicago computer's functions onto its sisters. We could have had them shut it down, but we didn't want to make the Dumplings suspicious.

"Second: they could have managed without Doydoy—but they would have had to use their brains. So they struck out at anybody who could have helped them—and they've been striking out all their lives. They could have made use of Doydoy all those years if they'd respected anything but his raw power—but they couldn't let a cripple teach them.

"They missed their chance with LaVonne because she's a girl, and a dwarf—and again with Prester. They might have won him over if they'd tried—but he's a Negro . . . the only one. No-one who was different could be an equal of theirs. Thank your stars they were so dumb . . . think of what they might have been able to do operating just one level higher."

She shuddered. "I don't like to think of it. Where are they now?"

"In the Dump. It's the only place we had for them."

"Is it safe?"

He smiled. "Do you know how they got out of the Dump?"

"I never had time to ask."

"Doydoy got them to take a whole lot of junk, compact it till it was extremely small and dense, heavier than lead, and pk it at one of the antennas. It hit and knocked it out of phase for a second, and the second was all they needed to get through the hole in the Field."

"That was pretty smart."

"That's what I told Doydoy, and all he said was, 'It took me eight years.' " He shook his head. "They won't do it again. We've got another circuit running around outside that one, and they'd never be able to manage it with two."

"Prester—"

"We wanted him to stay here with us, but he said he'd help us only if he could still live with the Aaslepps." Urquhart took out a cigar.

She didn't blame Prester. He had a place and wanted to keep it. She was trying to work up courage to ask about Doydoy when she noticed the band on Urquhart's cigar. "That's not a Sorrel Park homemade."

"No, thank God." He admired it for a moment. "Sorrel Park's opening up . . . on the Fourth of July"—he smiled wryly—"to celebrate the end of independence."

"Why?"

He shrugged. "After that donnybrook in Chicago there

wasn't much we could keep secret any more . . . I guess
people here will be happy enough. Stuff's coming in on a
use-it-now-pay-God-knows-when plan . . . that's how I got
the cigars. There's plenty of noise going on in the world
about us."

"I don't know . . . that Nigeria thing . . ."

"That'll be something to look forward to, all right, but now
everybody's playing cards close to the chest. They're perfectly happy to let us have the notoriety. You'll see, we'll
replace Middletown, Plainville and the Trobriand Islands in
all the learned journals."

"Sounds like endsville to me—but you won't let anybody
near the Dump."

"No." He added grimly. "And that'll be hardest of all."

She touched his hand. "You'll be leaving. You'll be out
of it, and it won't bother you."

He looked away and puffed in silence for a moment.
"There's a nice new uniform hanging in my closet. Maybe
I'll get up the nerve to put it on tomorrow, or the next
day . . ." He sighed. "It seems I'm free to leave, but I can't
. . . not because I didn't finish the job, but because I never
properly got started. Now I'll have more money, more help,
new ideas. And maybe I'll be able to do something. Anyway,
I'm getting married tomorrow."

"You are!"

"It's nice to see your face lighting up a bit! Yes, to Wilma
French, at the library. So you see, I'm stuck here."

Stuck here. He wasn't the only one with ambivalent feelings. *And after dark/ in Sorrel Park/ what will become of
me, me, me?*

"What's the matter, Shandy? Don't you approve of my
choice?"

"Dr. Urquhart, was all that true—about me?"

He said lightly, "It may not be exactly true, but it's
probably as near as makes no difference."

"I don't like it."

"Why?"

"It's scary."

"Not as bad as having psi."

"But I don't like it. What will happen to me?"

"Shandy, it's not even a theory—it's a belief. Nobody can
prove it one way or the other, so nobody will bother you too
much about it, or make the kind of fuss they're making about
psi. We know you're good, but we don't know what you're

good for yet. We might send you away for some testing and a little formal education to find out if we can make use of you around here—now you're looking really sick!"

"I'm sorry. I don't want to spoil things for you."

"You were searching so many years before you came here . . . but after you'd been here a while, I had the feeling you'd stopped. Maybe I can guess why. But Shandy, you did have to find out."

"Just for this," she said bitterly.

"You couldn't want anything better. You said so yourself. And it impresses me more than all the psi in the world." He stood up. "Now get dressed and sit out in the sunshine for a few minutes." He paused at the door. "You can see Marsh, too. He's been asking for you."

She confronted her face in the mirror. It was pale, and there were dark smudges under her eyes. It looked neither nobler nor wiser. "Hey, Odd Johnson!" she jeered, "where's your coltish grace?"

Her old clothes were missing from the closet. Someone had shopped for her: sandals, underwear, hair-ribbons, and a simple sleeveless white cotton dress with geometric designs— for Sorrel Park a marvel of taste and elegance. She dressed conscientiously but without spirit and walked out down the hall.

The place seemed quiet and empty. Then she heard voices and her heart leaped. Through an open door she could see Grace and Doydoy sitting in armchairs, talking to each other. She watched them for a moment with no desire to interrupt their private current of love and joy; she was satisfied that they had it.

Marczinek's door was closed. That was a different matter. Jason might express a hope by digging a flowerbed, but nothing so simple would relieve her feelings.

She had opened the strongbox of her emotions and delivered them into the hands of others—Marczinek was one of those others. If he died now when she had only just learned to love, and loved him so. . . . She did not even want to see him.

Jason was exercising his muscles with obvious pleasure, and singing as he mixed loam with topsoil:

Sew on that button, baby, patch up them shoes,

Sew on that button, put a patch on them old shoes;
Might as well be singin' jailbird blues . . .

He paused to mop his brow. "Go on, ask me why I'm not using psi for this." He spread a piece of sacking on the grass and she sat on it.

"Mesomorphs are active types."

"Tsk. Thought I'd get a rise out of you."

"You will," she said darkly. She sat there full of gloom, wishing she could take pleasure in the sunshine and the fresh new dress blowing about her legs. "You never did ask me what Margaret Mead would have done."

He leaned on the shovel. "Didn't have to. You were doing it all the time."

"Doing what?"

"Observing," he said simply. "Remember? New insight—"

"Don't!"

He shrugged. "All right—but one last question. Why are you trying to pick a fight? I saw it on your face the minute you looked out of the window."

"I'm not. I—I'm just upset about—Marczinek, and—and—" And myself.

"Then go and give Urquhart an earful!"

"I can't. He's getting married and I can't spoil things for him. And you—"

His eyes blazed. "I don't have any day to spoil? I don't have any feelings to hurt? I'm not sensitive, I sing because I'm an animal!"

"I didn't mean that, I—" She began to cry.

"Bawling again! God, I wish I could read you! No. No, I don't. You'd be just like all the rest, and I thought you were different."

"I am different. I'm too different." She burst into a new freshet. "I thought I'd be with everybody again—after all these years—and—and now I've just been kicked upstairs and pushed out!"

"Pushed out! Jeez, you take my breath away." He squatted on his heels beside her. "Is that all that's bugging you?"

"I don't want Marsh to die."

"Shandy, he's an old man, and he's hurt and tired. He feels he's had a good life, and he doesn't owe it to you to hang on just because you love him. You'll have to learn to depend on yourself all over again—but in a different way. It doesn't mean we're pushing you out. Don't disappoint us.

Marsh said you wouldn't turn down a good thing." He produced a handkerchief out of the air and she used it gratefully.
"Urquhart said all this was bothering you and I told him you
were too smart to get upset over it."

"You were wrong," she sniffled.

"I'm not wrong now. You better listen to me, because you
weren't listening to yourself very well when you were explain-
ing everything to Urquhart so lucidly and sensibly. Now
you've gotten all slewed round again. You think being a
supernormal means fighting crime from your secret mountain
fortress, emerging only to stop a runaway roller coaster—
like somebody in a comic-book? Afraid you'll be kept in a
glass case on a wad of cotton batting, or"—his tone became
gentle—"scared you'll die an old maid from waiting around
to find another supernormal to marry?"

"Yes," she said in a small voice.

"Gee whiz, Shandy, you said yourself what your kind of
person is for—to transfuse interesting and valuable new genes
into humanity—and in the meantime you can't be sure the
strain's transmissible, or even know for certain how to recognize another supernormal! So stop worrying. Look, suppose
in seven or eight years some honest and earnest-looking kook
came along and said"—he placed a hand on his breast and
proffered an imaginary bunch of flowers—" 'Shandy, will
you do me the honor of becoming my wife?'—would you
say"—he struck an even more ridiculous pose—" 'Nay, sir,
I cannot, for a higher destiny beckons, and I must follow
where it leads'?"

She giggled. "No, I'd only want to know—"

"What his IQ was!"

"That'd be nice to know, but I'd—"

"Ask to see his bankbook!"

"I'd just want to be sure he loved me, you goof!"

He stopped and looked at her. As though he were a
precog reaching there for the future, toward the matured
Shandy, she hoped: for wisdom and compassion, sexual
attractiveness, perhaps even a modest kind of beauty. He
said, "I think he'll manage that without too much trouble,"
and tweaked her nose. "Now please: wash the tears off your
face, say hello to Marsh, and get some more rest, or Grace
will give me hell . . . and on the way back, take a look in
the library. There's something worth seeing there, and I'm
not sure how long it's gonna be around."

She left, and he turned back to his garden and his song:

Sorrel Park fence, barb'wire go roun' an' roun',
Damn ol' fence, barb'wire go roun' an' roun';
Plane passin' over got a lonesome soun' . . .

The Dump was a closed and fortified place, but all doors were open where it was administered. She stood in the doorway of the library and confronted Curtis Quimper. He was bandaged around the ribs. One arm jutted at a strange angle because it was encased up to and around the shoulder in heavy plaster, and he had a shirt buttoned loosely about him.

He had helped and been rewarded; someone had kept her promise. The reward was perhaps disproportionate to the act, but then he had never done anything worth rewarding in his life, and the act was immensely significant. He looked up at her.

He had not been reading, or doing anything except sit and stare. There was no sense of reward on his face. They stared at each other, black hair, sallow skin, pointed faces, blue eyes, from opposite poles of humanity.

"How are you, Curtis?"

His eyes flashed, his mouth twisted as though he were about to flare up, but after a second the impulse died. Perhaps because he was being watched—or perhaps he was even trying to live up to freedom. His one thoughtless good deed would cost him many an indulgence.

But he only shrugged and said, "Lonely."

She shook her head and sighed. "Bro-ther, you aren't the only one!"

THE END

of an Original Gold Medal Novel

BY PHYLLIS GOTLIEB